Behind t

Peter Middleton

Behind the Fence.

Contents.

Precursor: The Prince is disturbed.

    1.   *The Discovery*

Precursor 2: The Prince decides.

    2.   *Government*
    3.   *Professor Frank Farley II*
    4.   *Press Release*

The Bomb

    5.   *The view behind the fence*
    6.   *The Professor*
    7.   *Questions, Questions, Questions*

Mr Waters Amazing Counting Machine.

    8.   *The Presidents dream*
    9.   *Marshall grows up*
    10.   *Return behind the fence*

Liberty

    11.   *The build*

The French

    12.   *Changing the skyline*
    13.   *The grand opening*

Petrol

    14.   *Revelation*
    15.   *Franks reaction*
    16.   *Departure & delivery*
    17.   *Looking sideways at home.*

Epilogue: 100000 years in the making.

For Mum.

You always believed I could do this.

Precursor

The Prince is disturbed

The Prince was having a rare quiet morning away from all the hustle and bustle of Royal life. In his life a rare moment to ones self was a luxury that could be ill afforded in the busy Royal household. He smiled to himself as he settled well into his old, brown, well-worn leather armchair, which was his personal favourite. This was quite an honour for this old armchair considering how many chairs there were in all the Royal palaces. He picked up his ironed copy of his favourite daily broadsheet newspaper and settled back for a read of the previous days worldwide events. The sun never sets on the British Empire and he would often find out about important events via the paragraphs of the free press quicker than the words from his many advisers.

In those settling moments as chair and man rapidly became one there was a harsh reminder of the world around him as his respite was disturbed by the loud rap of bare knuckles against the solid oak door.

Immediately he felt that this intrusion into his well-earned break was too much to bear as he shifted angrily in his seat, instantly making himself uncomfortable and a little agitated. The unwelcome intruder repeated his knock on the door, only this time a little louder, before the Prince had a chance to answer the first. He angrily threw his thick, heavy, broadsheet newspaper to the floor before standing.

"Enter!" he yelled, trying not to sound too angry but failing dismally.

The door slowly creaked open and a uniformed figure clumsily entered the room acting as if he felt that he shouldn't come in even though he had been invited, albeit rather harshly.

"Sorry to intrude your highness" the words stumbled out of General Lynnes' mouth as he positioned himself nervously in front of the now standing Prince whilst he offered up a clumsy, pointless salute.

"Well Lynne! What in Gods name do you want? Come on spit it out! Tell me why you have disturbed me?" responded the now more than agitated Prince, who fired off the questions quicker than the General could answer as he made it crystal clear that he hated nothing more than having his rare peaceful moments disturbed.

"We have had a message," the General rather clumsily said as he suddenly really wished he had sent someone else to do his dirty work.

"What sort of message do you see fit to disturb me with? Is it those pesky Europeans? I have warned them once to behave, are we under threat?" retorted a now concerned Prince as his brain rapidly considered all the usual scenarios that normally confronted him.

"Its not a threat, its more of a request an invitation of sorts" the General was feeling more confident now as he knew the Prince would be calmer as the conversation proceeded. He also knew the piece of paper in his hand had a message on it which could change the Princes and the Empires thinking forever.

"I had better look at it then" replied a now inquisitive Prince before he stretched out his hand and took the paper from the nervous General. He slowly unfolded the strange, waxy paper and slowly read the badly spelt hand written message.

The Prince tried to digest the message a couple of times before finally looking up from the letter and recommencing his icy stare towards the general.

"Is this some sort of fancy joke? Are you trying to lark around and waste my time?" yelled a now angrier than ever Prince, who hated wasting time with pointless jokes.

"No sir. It is genuine it has been verified and we are one hundred per cent sure this is a real and viable message… its amazing isn't it?" The General offered up the assessment of the message as if his very life depended on it.

The Prince looked at the General for any telling signs that this was just a jape, He saw none, the General was completely serious, his face set like stone. The Prince sat back down and dramatically slumped back into his chair. His brow was deep with shadowed furrows as he immediately went into deep thought. 'How could this be?' 'Where had it come from?' and 'Why?' these were the thoughts that whizzed around his head as he tried to summon up a plan for what could be the biggest event in history of the planet. After what seemed like a lifetime he looked up at the stern General who was still stood to attention in front of him.

"Call an emergency meeting of the cabinet and the heads of all our armed forces" he spoke softly as though he wasn't sure of who he was going to address this to or how he was going to explain it.

"Also all of the Empires top engineers as we need to get onto this immediately" added the Prince.

"Do you think it would be a good precaution to open the War Office?" asked General Lynne.

"Good thinking. We have no idea what they might have planned!" agreed the Prince before ushering the General away with his outstretched arm

The General scuttled out of the room much faster than he arrived as the Prince stood up and walked towards the fireplace, that was crackling with the sound of burning logs. He stood gazing into the fire for a moment before holding up the paper and taking a longer examination of the message. He ran his fingers over the paper and noted that it didn't feel right. It was much thicker than the high quality royal paper and there appeared to be a silk sheen over the writing. He held the message against the window to examine it against the evening sun, which shone down through the Palace window, and the watermark clearly depicted a map of the night sky. He also noticed that as he stared at the watermark it appeared to come alive with the stars slowly rotating around the page.

In his amazement the Prince turned and walked back across the room before slowly sitting back in his armchair. He sat for some time and kept reading the message to himself.

"This is going to be incredible," he quietly whispered to himself.

Chapter 1

The Discovery

Marshall was not a fan of Wednesday nights. This was not because there was nothing on television or the weather was bad but because it was pub night. Mum was working and dad would pack him into the car to go and 'see Grandad'.

'Going to see Grandad' was a curious statement, which always made Marshall smile. Normally all he saw of Grandad was his back as he walked into the pub, dutifully followed by his dad. Marshall would have to go around the back of the pub and play with the other boys and girls. He didn't really know any of theses children or go to school with them, but in those early years of the seventies everyone was a friend. The games here were fun and the sun always seemed to shine. There was never any anger or shouting and Marshall often used to think how it was a complete opposite to life within the pub. When the doors opened to the pub the children would all look up and listen to the shouting adults that were either enjoying a good joke or arguing over a game of dominoes.

Whilst his dad drank beer with his friends Marshall would play and drink his one solitary bottle of pop that tasted very little like the promised name on the label. If he was lucky he could look forward to a nice bag of crisps as well, but that would be it. Money wasn't sparse within his family but at the same time they were not flush. If the question was a bottle of pop or another pint of beer, the pint of beer would win, much to Marshall's disagreement. Luckily all the other children's parents thought in exactly the same way and therefore all the children would run out of pop at the same time, which was normally two to three minutes into the game.

Around the pub was what everyone liked to call 'The oval'. 'The oval' was a garden surrounded by a twenty-foot high-sloped bank. The overall radius of 'the oval' must have been two hundred feet and all along the ridge past a short path was a metal fence. The panels of the fence were padlocked together and held in place over it were thick black sheets which did a more than effective job of destroying any possible view beyond the border.

Marshall had asked his father many times what was behind the fence and he was content with the standard reply of a 'pit that went wrong', enough for the curious mind who was more interested in the game of tic. A bizarre game, which, to Marshall just seemed to involve one child being 'on' and proceed to chase the other children to 'capture' them. All of his friends loved being part of this ongoing and seemingly endless game and as quickly as it finished another game would start. The fence would often become part of the games they played, either as a den or a safe area in which you could catch your breath. No one ever tried to climb it or vandalise it, which in the days of graffiti, anarchy and punk rock seemed more than a little odd to Marshall.

The fence had been there for many years and looked like it would be there for many more. Its appearance had never changed in Marshall's eyes. It had started to show some signs of aging around the edges but in general it served its purpose well, no more than a limit for the pub garden and the children's imaginary games, all of which was fine in Marshalls mind.

Marshall was never the most adventurous of children but for as long as he could remember he had been very happy in his own little world. He was always careful around new people and to many this would come over as being shy, but Marshall wasn't shy he was just thoughtful and would only speak if he had something sensible to say. What people didn't realise was that all the time Marshall was quietly in his mind creating situations that he would have to solve, with his treasured toys, at home.

This could be building new roads and buildings or dreaming up problems, with ever more extreme loads, for his toy lorries and cranes.

This particular sun drenched evening Marshall was sat alone at the top of the bank looking down at the old pub and although he was somewhat lonely, he was far from bored. It was the school summer holidays and he had spent a good part of the day engineering a move for his mum's old black sewing machine. It could have just been carried across the room but for Marshall to get the most enjoyment from his day it would have to be moved by means of his many toys. The multitude of toys that Marshall had accrued over many birthdays and Christmas's were practically all involved. Police cars lined the route as did toy soldiers, pen lids were lined across the carpet and made very effective road cones. The old sewing machine had been dragged onto the back of an old indestructible toy lorry and trailer, that could accommodate the weight, but there were problems with the turn half way across the room.

This, and many other problems that Marshall was perusing at great depth whilst lying alone on the bank, soaking in the early evening sun. The air was perfectly still and the weather was fine, for late July, the grass was badly mowed but green and dust had settled on the cinder path on top of the bank. In the immediate area he could hear the general noise from the pub and the occasional laughter. The road in front of the pub would occasionally offer a car, which would break the stillness with its revving petrol engine.

After a short time Marshall decided enough was enough and lay back on the grass that felt slightly damp but warm and comfortable. He lay motionless staring at the clouds for a while taking occasional sips from his drink that was labelled 'cola' but tasted more like warm, soapy bath water. Marshall looked back at the old fence wondering if one day it would come down and if not who looked after it. The fence was getting a little worse for wear in parts and he wondered when anyone came to maintain it. Perhaps they came in the day when the pub was closed or, as he liked to think, it was maintained at night when everyone was asleep because the government could not allow anyone to see the secrets behind.

He lay there for what seemed like an eternity staring into space and half thinking about the fence and half thinking about the Russian air force base right behind the fence which would burst into life at any moment staging a full on invasion of England, this made him laugh to himself as he thought at least he would have a good seat of which to view the impending war.

Marshall glanced down at the pub thinking it would be nice to get a fresh drink but there were no signs of life. He proceeded to lazily look around the oval noting its perfection; this fact alone made him stop for a moment. He had never noticed how perfectly oval it really was and the pub, which was a very odd looking building, was right in the middle. In fact it was perfectly in the middle he concluded as he continued to slowly survey the area. The triangular red roof of the pub, which reminded him of the dials on his Granddads cooker, pointed directly back at him like a huge arrow directing the way. The pub was triangular in shape as well. This was all new to his eyes as the only thing previously that building had ever been good for was pop and crisps and meeting his Wednesday night friends. 'What an odd building in a lovely semi circle of earth' he thought. Marshall imagined from the sky it would look like a huge cooker control, not the new ones but the old cookers with huge Bakelite controls. Marshalls imagination was now racing with all sorts of mad ideas. Perhaps it was a pointer for the Russian bombers to guide them home? or it pointed directly north for people in hot air balloons with no compasses? Marshall giggled to himself as he even thought of Aliens landing in the pub garden. Now he was getting restless and a little bit bored. His dad would be drinking and talking for hours to come and all of the cheap and nasty pop was gone, just leaving a sticky residue in the bottom of the bottle that would soon attract the local insects.

"Probably no crisps tonight either" Marshall said to himself.

With this hungry thought in mind Marshall started to meander about the oval occasionally looking up at the fence. After walking from one end of the garden to the other he made a swift turn and started to return to his resting place when he spotted a gap.

Marshall stood frozen to the spot.

He felt like he had broken it and was about to be reprimanded by his dad for doing yet another thing wrong. He stood perfectly still and listened to the breath entering and exiting his lungs as he tried to figure out what to do next. He could just ignore it and walk on pretending it wasn't there, and continuing with his thoughts of sewing machine moving, or he could have a look. After all it was only a 'pit that had gone wrong', perhaps an embarrassment for the Coal Board, but not exactly a national secret! Then his mind began to wander as he thought perhaps it was something more sinister, like the soviets building an airbase!

In his heart he knew that there was only one way to find out, and that would be to climb through and have a look, but he was way too scared so he walked straight past the gap and pretended he hadn't seen it.

Marshall walked all the way round to the other side of the garden and tried his best not to look at the fence.

"Marshall" came the loud cry in that deep Derbyshire accent that he knew so well

" Pop!" came the second shout as Marshall finally caught his dad's gaze and waved. His dad didn't wait for Marshall to even move before he waved back and disappeared back into the pub. Marshall ran to the table grabbing the fizzy pink drink that tasted nothing like 'bubble gum' as promised on the label. He took a great big gulp of pop and whilst his head was tipped back his eye was drawn back to the gap in the fence.

He really wished he had never seen it. For he knew that his brain would not forget it, he wasn't that type of person, it would lodge in his sub-conscious and he knew it would nag at him whenever he relaxed.

In his mind he made an immediate and rash decision, there was only one thing for it, he would have to go through the gap and have a look. Marshall was not and had never been a brave child. Most films that were even half scary would be avoided like the plague and even a television programme that hinted at ghosts or anything remotely supernatural was to be avoided. Fear is a powerful emotion and behind the fence he may have to confront his greatest fear, it might just be very dark. He didn't like to admit it but an extreme fear of the dark is no fun at all, often he would spend all day dreading 'bedtime'.

'Up the wooden hill!', his dad would shout, and Marshall would go upstairs and lie in bed for the next two hours desperately trying to sleep.

'Just shut your eyes and go to sleep' he would be told by his loving mother, but how can you when doing that causes the one thing you are scared of?

The fence presented a massive dilemma for Marshall and his young brain. In one hand he wanted to go and look through the gap and on the other he didn't want any part of it because it scared him to death. He then thought about waiting until the next visit when he could bring a case full of tools for exploring, but what could happen in the meantime? Apart from thinking about the fence night and day, some one else might find the gap and discover a secret Russian base! Foil the enemy and be a hero like the ones he read about in one of his many books and comics. Pride is also very strong emotion and Marshall knew that if someone else looked first he would forever feel like he had lost out on fame and fortune. At this moment a thought broke into his conscious that didn't help at all. Every time he had been to the pub there had been loads of children playing everywhere, but, today there were none.

This thought sent his vivid imagination into overdrive.

Had a monster behind the fence eaten them all? Or had they found the gap and ran all the way home to get their own exploration kits? Would he let them beat him to the greatest discovery of the cold war? Could he let this happen? Would he get eaten?

The thoughts fired like exploding fireworks in his brain as he stood staring at the gap whilst finishing the last of the disgusting pop that seemed to last forever. He made the decision that he would have to look. It could not wait; he could not risk missing out on the fame of being known as 'The Child explorer who stopped an invasion'. He could already envisage his face on the front of the papers and his mothers smile as she stood at Buckingham Palace collecting her medal for having such a brilliant son. She was so proud of his achievements at school already so he could only imagine her admiration for this discovery. Also the thankful drinkers who have been saved from certain death who would embellish him with drinks, crisps and sweets.

It was all too much and he finally made his decision. He would have to look right now.

Marshall slowly walked up the slope and kept his eyes firmly fixed on the gap; if anything jumped out he could get back to the pub quick. With this in mind he walked around the edge of the oval not quite on the cinder path, as he had convinced himself that the slope would give him a head start over anything that could spring out of the gap. He stood opposite the gap for a good five minutes before stepping forward looking at the fence. He noted one of the padlocks had rusted away and the fence had fallen forward slightly, allowing him access. He stepped forward and slowly squeezed through the gap.

What he saw next took his breath away.

Precursor 2

The Prince decides.

The Prince gathered all his top officials and military spokesmen into the grand hall at Buckingham Palace. The room was full of all the brightest and most qualified people that the British Empire could muster all waiting expectantly for the arrival of the Prince.

Upon his arrival everyone stood and bowed to the most powerful of men, to which immediately he told them to stop being so silly and let him commence his speech.

"We the British have been contacted by a race of people from the stars who wish us to build a landing platform right here in the magnificent city of London" barked a confident Prince.

The room fell into complete silence as he tried to hold his nerve through the rest of the speech.

"The plans for this device have been beamed to us through space and time to land right here in London at Downing Street. I know it is genuine, as I have seen it with my own eyes. They have asked us to build a huge steel and glass structure, bigger than any other constructed in order for them to land their vessel here and share with us the benefit of their incredible skills and knowledge. And I am sure I do not need to add the incredible value of these advances to this great nation, we will have knowledge and weapons beyond our wildest dreams. Another added benefit will be that no other country, within our Empire or any other, will dare to question our military strength with this incredible ally on board."

"The plans are available now for your perusal and we will need to build this structure within nine months in order for this alien race to land here and share their resources and knowledge with us. I will personally oversee the construction and will ensure that any required resources are available for the building to be completed. Cost is not a worry"

"Gentlemen", the Prince added as he looked around the room, "Failure is not an option!"

"Any questions?" asked the Prince; quietly hoping that no one would ask any.

"Sir, how will the public react?" asked a rather flushed looking gentleman at the front of the meeting room.

"They do not need to know what its for! They will do as we say. I will personally promote the building as an exhibition of all the worlds' goods and our achievements as an Empire, a sort of trades show if you like. I am sure that the public will love it and come from far and wide to see the many fascinating exhibits. This will generate an income for the project and also provide perfect cover for us, as in the meantime we can get the building ready for the landing!"

"What's this building going to be called?" asked a rather large red-faced general

"I have called it the Crystal Palace," replied a confident Prince. With this he rolled out the plans on the front table. They were far ahead of their time as the plans were designed on computers and were printed on white computer paper, a fact that on its own drew gasps of awe from the eager crowd.

The work on planning the construction of this magnificent structure commenced immediately after the meeting. The list of people wishing to work on this fantastic and fanciful project was seemingly endless list of all the top engineers and designers of the age. Unusual for this group of people was the fact that no one ever questioned the Princes words, it would seem that whatever he wanted he got and the construction would be built on this principle. The only requirement of all the people in the room that day was that they had to sign the official secrets act relating to any information they had seen. The signed documents were placed in the most secret basement of Buckingham Palace along with every document that would never be revealed to the public.

The crowd of engineers and designers were split into teams, depending on their expertise that could drive the project forward quickly and efficiently. The groundwork for this development was to start immediately and the building was to be erected at a speed previously unheard of in Victorian times.

Within nine months the Crystal Palace was built on the exact coordinates detailed on the messages and to the exact specification of the alien plans. The building represented a magnificent demonstration of cutting edge engineering and the public was constantly in awe of the incredible men who built this fantastic show. The trades show opened that same year to worldwide applause and appreciation of the effort that had gone into its construction. The show was a roaring success with thousands of members of the public visiting every day. This, along with the small entrance fee, ensured that the show was very profitable and more than covered the cost of the vastly expensive building.

The Prince and everyone involved in this project were now ready for the landing. They were all aware of how it would progress the mighty British Empire onto total world domination. These thoughts were dashed when, only a week before the proposed landing, a note arrived at Downing Street.

Even though the Prince and his team had achieved so much, in so little time, they were now been asked to do more.

It wasn't going to happen and the building had to be moved.

The message arrived at Downing Street like a shot to the Princes' heart as the need to move this structure would need him to convince everyone it was a good idea.

The only good news is that they had a couple of years to do it in, as there were problems on the other planet that would cause a delay. The exhibition continued to be a success and, as planned, closed later that year. As per the alien instructions the palace was moved, much to the publics' surprise, to a new location within the time span. To help to cover these additional costs it was then opened as a museum. Meanwhile the messages from this new race continued and everyone involved waited patiently.

On the new date for the landing the atmosphere in the Palace was incredible. Everyone who knew what was about to happen was excited that this new power was coming today and Britannia would rule the world with its new ally and powerful new weapons.

That night they all stood outside the Crystal Palace as nothing happened at all. After waiting for a further two hours the Prince resigned himself to the fact that the others would not be coming and made his way back to the Palace, a broken man. At this very time the now familiar noises of static electricity were echoing around Downing Street as a note arrived which the Prime Minister eagerly picked up before reading:

'We are sorry. We failed in our mission. As some way of an apology we have sent you some plans for items that you haven't discovered yet, please use them wisely. We are recalculating the transmission and will contact you very soon

Kindest regards and apologies

Frank Farley II'

What followed in the rest of the message was an equation explaining the splitting of the atom and genetic engineering. Two designs and equations that wouldn't be deciphered for at least another two hundred years.

There was also a design for an advanced visual talking machine, which meant that two people in different places could communicate via the airwaves and also send each other pictures. An Italian scientist took particular interest in these plans and commenced work on them immediately.

Many years later on a winters night the Crystal Palace burnt down in a totally unexplained fire, which could be seen for many miles around and shocked all of London at its intensity. Some five hundred fire-fighters fought the blaze for two days with many of them being overcome by the intense furnace of flames. Members of the general public, who came from far and wide, lined the streets of Sydenham; to witness the destruction of one of most loved structures in the capital.

The fire was researched by the Fire Brigade and the Police but marked down as unexplained. Unexplained that was to everyone but the surviving members of the original team, who knew exactly what had happened. The flight and landing had taken place, albeit eighty years late, and they had built the palace in exactly the right place and to the right design but the alien race had once again failed in its mission. On re-entry to our dimension and arriving at the landing site the craft had failed at the incredible power of the flight coming to an end. This had resulted in the ship, and all its helpless occupants, exploding in mid-flight and appearing inside the building as a ball of flame. It was this ball of flames that landed inside the Crystal Palace on that fateful night. This immediately started a chain reaction of events that destroyed the magnificent building with an uncontrollable fire and repeated unexplained explosions.

This may have been another set back in the others plans to link the two planets but they were determined to get this right. Mankind would be a valuable and interesting friend who they could help to develop for a better future.

Chapter 2

Government

"Well I am not increasing interest rates! So find other answers!" the words echoed around the room as the telephone receiver was jettisoned onto its holder with such force that a lesser-made machine would buckle under the pressure.

President Toppleton had been in post for less than one day and already the pressure of running the biggest nation on the planet was beginning to tell. After winning the election he had taken up the reins of a runaway economy that had lurched and bucked its way into recession like a wild horse that would not be tamed. It seemed to him that no one really knew how to get out of the mess, that had been left by his forefathers, and the tried and tested methods just didn't work anymore.

Having won a landslide victory he now wondered why he had ever tried to get himself in this high-pressure position. He had promised the people of America that he and his team would turn this country around and relive the fantastic days of yesteryear when the American dream was still intact. The election campaign had successfully sold the idea that he was the best candidate to the masses with his catch all slogan of 'Out with the old and in with the new'. It was his own personal sideswipe at previous governments who had no idea how to change anything and just seemed to lurch from one crisis to another. New President, new rules and new advisors were all the public wanted but unfortunately not all was rosy in the garden. The simple truth is that no matter how good new ideas seemed when you dream them up actually implementing them into public life is a whole different matter. The ugly beast that is known as financial pressure doesn't ever sleep and it brings with it a whole host of colleagues, unemployment, depression and war. The latter causing him more than a few sleepless nights as the nations of the world continued to bicker over the decreasing, and ever more valuable, natural resources. His country alone had stood out as a self-titled 'World Police', a very noble gesture but incredibly expensive. The cost was not only counted in dollars but the horrendous amount of body bags that returned from all over the globe every week.

He was determined to do something to help his people but he just couldn't move for problems and fear. This fear was like nothing he had ever felt and raised its head every time he had to make a major decision.

He sat back in the Oval Office and looked at the photographs of his predecessors and he couldn't help but feel a little jealous. They had all the resources they needed to do whatever the public wanted. They could start a space race or prop up a car industry with one flick of the pen over a seemingly never-ending amount of blank cheques. He had no money and the public would only keep faith with him for so long before questions of his abilities would be asked. The public wanted only one thing, and this had become blindingly apparent through the many polls during the elections, and this was to get out of this recession and start building the future. The public wanted the future that they had always been promised.

The President got up and walked to his drinks cabinet and slowly poured himself an ice-cold glass of cola. As he sipped at the drink he couldn't help himself from remembering his childhood and the emotions that had driven him to become a politician. He started to reminisce over the early years of his life that were spent building ever more fantastic model spaceships. These designs were the ones that he dreamt in the future would be able to move mankind away from this planet and help us to populate the solar system. He would show his father the many plans he had drawn and describe how in the future he would rule America and they would be built. As the years passed he would sit with his father who would tell him how the space race had ended because it was expensive and no one was interested anymore. The financial implications of space travel would be slowly explained to him and he would question why we could spend money on tanks but not rockets. His father would laugh and try to explain national security, the implications of invasions and the Communists faults for starting the Cold War, he would listen intently but would not accept any of it. In his little mind his machines were the best and he was determined that in the future they would be built.

As the years passed and he got older the fanciful spaceships were replaced by architecture and his love of buildings. This inevitably led him to mix with others with similar interests and armed him with more questions to ask. At the age of just fourteen he was representing his local party for election of the towns mayor, his political journey started and the dreams of spaceships died. The many hundreds of his drawings and models were assigned to the trash whilst his interest in running the country gathered momentum. One day he knew he would be President but in the deepest recesses of his memory he had never forgotten the basis of why he wanted to do it in the first place.

He did have a plan.

His dream was to get into politics and eventually be in a position of extreme power, being President afforded him this luxury. His plan was to simply repair the economy and then to relaunch the space program. He would establish the space program and then try to build the machines, which had driven his imagination as a child. The government would then give the public back some of the dreams that they had been promised over many years of mis-management.

The plan was that simple in his head before he became President.

Since he had become President the harsh reality had hit him like an express train. The economy would take years to repair and the various conflicts over the globe which his great country were involved in were draining the money from the economy like water draining from a bathtub. The space program had effectively died in the seventies after the last moon landing had been nothing more than an after thought on the evening news and it would take years, and vast resources, to build up again. It would take a very brave or foolish President to increase taxes in order to fund a select few individuals the privilege of going into orbit. The public viewed the whole space race as an expensive folly that had afforded some a magical experience and global fame, which they had paid for from their hard work and toil back on Earth. Successive governments had promised the wonders of a new space program but, with the exception of a now unmanned orbiting space station, none had delivered any kind of sustained programme of development. The people had wanted to explore the stars and thoughts of manning other planets always excited adults and children alike, but the harsh reality is that its very expensive and no one wants to pay. It had been fifty years since the moon landings had grabbed mankind's imagination and, with the exception of a few brief flirtations with our near space, that was it. Man had raced to the moon and stopped at that.

'One small step for man' was a step too far for the many finance houses.

Money had once again stopped the dream. The shareholders and investors of the day simply asked the question; 'What is in it for us?' and the answers they received from the men in power was 'Not a lot!'. However if they asked the same question about weapons development they received a very different and favourable response. The governments of the day realised very quickly that the Apollo missions were not a long-term vote winner, but, the money from weapons sales provided a much-needed prop for the economy and plenty of money means happy voters. When the Apollo missions finally stopped hardly anyone in the public noticed.

That was no one except for a little boy in Chicago who stared at the stars every night and dreamt of exploring the Galaxy. He wanted to climb into his space ships and discover new worlds. These new worlds could be explored and mankind could benefit from their habitation and resources.

All those many years ago back then in the mid-seventies he had promised himself and his father that if he ever became President he would get rid of all the non-believers and build space ships to explore the universe.

The only issue now was that small boy with his big dreams did not have any fiscal skills. He didn't understand money and investors or any of the institutions that make the decisions to invest in these massively expensive projects. He sat alone in the Oval Office after all those years of dreaming and he was only now all too aware of the restraints that he was now subject to, his very political livelihood depended on them. The people had elected him, but it was the banks, which effectively ran the country.

It was these banks that had led the population into the worst recession in modern history. This recession had held the country in its icy grip for a decade and showed no signs of easing. The people of this once great country had seen their property and investments become worthless, whilst countless others had lost everything at the nod of a faceless stockbroker or bailiffs who they would never meet. In contrast to recessions of old this one had handed out no favours, some very big and once powerful companies had ceased to exist and had taken some very good people with them. The downturn had been relentless as every strategy had been attempted and exhausted in attempts to pull the out of it, by a parade of failed politicians. Every government since had blamed someone else whether it be the Eighties excess, the Nineties overspending, or the Noughties disregard for everything except profit. To keep firing blame at others was aimless but one thing was now blatantly clear to this man who used to dream, He had been elected by the people to sort it out. He alone was at the helm of a country, which had been sailing aimlessly through a terrible storm and now the people needed clear direction. They wanted answers and he would have to provide them.

He needed these answers and he needed them quickly. He had promised the public change and now he needed to deliver.

He looked around the room and wondered if any of his predecessors had ever felt so small and useless. He envied the previous Presidents who had promised so much to the public, often with no intention of delivering, and how they had been applauded and respected by their individual generations. They had continuously sold the dream with ever more elaborate and fanciful schemes, which more often than not came to absolutely nothing. They sold the dream that we were going to be better and before they could fail they had retired or moved on to other things.

We were going to live in fantastic futuristic houses in crime free cities that would be criss-crossed by flying cars. The houses would be filled with every gadget and machine to make our lives better and work would become a thing of the past, as mass automation would take care of all the mundane tasks, which had haunted mankind for a millennia. They would help to sell this via huge Worlds Fairs, which would dominate a town or country that they were in for at least a year. These fairs of old would attract millions of visitors who would explore the attractions and discover what life would be like in the future for them and their children. These were normal hard working families that saw the dream, were promised it by the government of the day, and they wanted it. They fought off recession in these early days of the nineteen hundreds by working longer and harder with the belief that one day life would be better. The governments of the day promised if they worked hard, and fendered off recession, then those dreams would materialise.

As he stood and finished his drink, the President couldn't help but get a little angry at how all the previous governments had sold the dream over and over and over again, only to never deliver any of the promises that had been so blatantly displayed. We had slowly started to look inwards rather than reaching for the stars and he couldn't help thinking that this was the reason that this recession had failed to lift for so long. The public no longer believed that the government knew where to go next. The dream had been diluted so far that it was no more than a notion rather than something to work towards.

The media had done a superb job of instilling fear into generation of working people. Fear of losing your home, fear of unemployment, fear of your kids not having the latest fashions and fear of failure. This did a great job of keeping everyone looking inwards and had instilled fear for so long that it had made the daily grind of life on earth a very depressing reality for billions of her occupants. In an attempt to reduce the pension bills some countries had done away with retirement altogether, presenting the workingman with a means of working till he dropped. The public didn't need any help in realising that this was no dream at all. A long and happy retirement was everyone's right and these successive governments had even stolen that.

The President moved to the front window of his office and studied that allowed him a panoramic view of the White House lawns and the busy road in front. He could see the protestors, that had been a regular feature for so long that most people thought they were a permanent, and couldn't help but feel some common ground between them. He could quite happily stand and demonstrate at the lack of caring that had been shown by generations of politicians.

With these thoughts of protest ringing in his head he summoned his Vice-President for a conversation.

Graham Hertog had been his friend and colleague since university. He trusted him more than any person on earth and often talked to him about new and mainly ridiculous ideas that he was having. He could always rely on him for an honest and fair answer. Graham also had a much firmer grip on the financial implications of whatever scheme was flying around and would be quick to point out if it was plausible.

After welcoming Graham in his office he offered him a drink and beckoned him to sit in the luxurious leather settees.

"I am thinking of introducing a Space Program" started a confident President.

"Not on the scale of our previous efforts but a smaller more economical model. What do you think?" he said whilst trying to maintain eye contact with a clearly flustered Graham.

"With all due respect, Mr President, we barely have enough money to pay the nurses and city workers. I do not think that we could even dream of trying to build a space program at this time…" Grahams words tailed off as he saw the President rise out of his seat.

"But surely we could appeal to business leaders to help us to build this. I think it would bode well with the working man," replied the President who already knew he was losing this brief exchange.

"We would be slaughtered by the business community for even attempting to talk about this, these companies are struggling to pay wages and all but essential spending is suspended. The public would think that we have lost our marbles and have us quickly removed from governing. It would be political suicide" replied Graham in his usual straight talking and assertive manner, before continuing, " The money simply is not there and the public will not buy into an expensive folly whilst they are fighting to feed themselves and their families."

"What if we suspend military action in some parts?" injected the President.

"You would save some money, but the debts we have got would swallow any small saving," replied Graham as he sipped at his drink.

"What about if I suspend them all?"

"You would save a lot of money and lives. I am not sure of the exact amounts but it would be massive. The only problems I foresee are what happens to the conflict zones? And what do we do with all the military personnel?"

"We could stop half the conflicts and no-one would notice and the personnel could be used on other things!" said a confident President.

"You would be a brave man indeed", said Graham before the President closed their brief exchange.

The President stood and stared out the windows. He knew Graham was right, he always was, and the sadness still swept through him as he realised that whichever way he turned he couldn't find a simple answer to his problem.

He was never going to be able to build his space ships.

With this last thought of his political day he felt another part of his boyhood dreams and ambitions die at the cruel hands of reality.

Chapter 3

Professor Frank Farley

Dreaming dreams is easy, turning those dreams into reality was Franks job. He worked in a large laboratory, which was paid for by the state, and he personally managed a team of some two hundred scientists and engineers. They were regularly tasked, by the public, with building ever more complex designs and ideas. These developments would transform people's lives and make the planet a more comfortable place for everyone.

For over two hundred years the department had thought of, developed and manufactured every conceivable machine and gadget, some new and some just improvements on previous ideas. Every idea would be fully researched and the solution would be tested before being released onto the public domain.

Frank had started work as a shy but eager sixteen year old. He had developed in his early years a firm grasp of the laws of physics, quantum mechanics, mathematics and advanced problem solving. Those first few years at work were very tough, as he had to repeatedly prove himself to his now retiring boss, Professor Hans Michigan. Michigan had been at the forefront of developing many great ideas that had revolutionized transport and communication throughout the globe. Frank had for the last two decades desperately tried to step out of his mentors' long and rather imposing shadow. This had proved incredibly difficult for Frank as everything Hans seemed to touch turned to gold, ideas others had laughed at, or were unable to develop, were rapidly turned into reality and the population would then realize they couldn't live without them. When Michigan finally decided to retire it would be Franks unenviable job to ensure that the department continued to develop ideas that could be adopted and loved by the public.

Frank always knew in his heart that this would be no mean feat.

Michigan's only lasting nemesis was space travel. It was the single subject that interested him the most and the one that caused him the most headaches. Since he had designed the machines that had conquered the Moon, he had become somewhat disillusioned by the publics ignorance at the requirement to go further. What made the task of selling the idea to the masses harder was the amount of terrible disasters that had followed since those exciting first steps away from the planet. The excessive funding had always been in place for research into deep space travel as any government could see that it was the future, and it could bring unknown rewards. It could also provide their biggest adventure and everyone needed an adventure.

Franks earlier days at the grandly named 'Department for Ideas and Development' were spent developing better observation equipment of space and distant stars. The machines and telescopes he helped to develop could look at stars and decide if there were planets circling those stars. This information could be processed to inform them if life could possibly be out there somewhere in the distant galaxies. This was incredibly complicated and hard work and it had cost Frank his first marriage and he would say his sanity, as Michigan's drive for more information consumed year after year of Franks' life. Many of the team considered it to be somewhat of a folly to find life among the stars, but dreams are dreams and the public wanted them to be fulfilled at all costs.

This lesson in dreams had been taught to Frank at a very early age when his father took him to the "Worlds Fair'33" his fondest memory as a child. This fair had developed his interest in science and technology and drove him to become a professor. He often told people of his great excitement at walking around this massive show where every nation showed its new technologies and its combined dreams for tomorrow. Some of these had remained dreams, for instance no one had developed a walking, talking man sized robot that could help around the house and make tea. That was a dream that had been continuously worked on for years but had proved to be far from viable. Others ideas had worked out better, he distinctly remembered going into a room and feeling incredibly cold for that hot July day, his father informed him it was 'air conditioning' and it would stay cool all year round in houses, cars and airplanes. At the time he wondered how this worked and who would buy it, but just a few years later it was everywhere and totally accepted as the norm.

Many car manufacturers of the day showed the cars of the future, ultra streamlined versions that promised smooth rides and incredible speed, most had been developed and looked little like those prototypes but worked all the same. These early days had led to massive jumps in the automotive industry and the department had more than played its part, developing better and more efficient engines, electric, hydrogen and even nuclear options (although the latter was considered too dangerous for normal families). Frank had often looked back when he was struggling with an idea or concept and tried to think how those earlier generations had dreamed up such fantastic contraptions. He found this a great way of spurring himself on to better things.

That Worlds Fair was designed to celebrate one hundred years of progress of one of the major cities in his country. After years of planning and building the Fair opened in May '33 to a fanfare of light and sound, indeed the nearest star had provided the opening beams of light to announce the show was open. Over the next year twenty two million people of all races would walk through the street of this magnificent exhibition of dreams and reality. If one so wished you could order a car in the morning of your arrival and watch it being built through the day, driving it home that night. This was the greatest show the planet had ever seen demonstrated by the public wanting more and more of it. The fair was planned originally for one year but due to incredible public demand it was back the following year with more attractions and wonders for the workingman to look at, so much so in total over fifty million people paid to view the wonders. He remembered this second year for his fathers ambition to ride on a huge cable car which had a view over the entire fair and his mother wanting to view the houses of the future, he often wondered how they would feel now he was in charge of the department responsible for bringing some of those dreams to life.

Frank had continued Michigan's early work on ideas that could make space travel possible. His early successes with his boss such as the moon landings had resulted in him being tasked with developing a returnable 'shuttle' which could service near orbit space stations. These stations would house experiments, living quarters and astronomy equipment, which could look further into space when free of the planets atmosphere and eventually, he hoped, holidays and space travel would be open to all. These first steps were taken cautiously as it was a complicated process requiring massive amounts of money, development and training. Those early astronauts were the film stars of their time, living the high life on and off the planet, but there was a price to pay for this luxury. The early rockets were very crude and unstable having to use massive amounts of fuel to propel them upward and break the gravitational pull of the planet. If it went wrong, as it often did, then it was like sitting on top of a huge bomb as a brave few found to their cost. To make things even worse taking off was only half the battle, the return journey was even more dangerous as the friction of the atmosphere tried to rip the spaceship and the astronauts to pieces. Those early disasters were classed as accidents but as time went on and more accidents happened it became blatantly obvious to everyone that this was not the most efficient way to travel into space.

Frank had designed a returnable shuttle that meant the same machine could be used time and time again with very little waste and hopefully provide a safer and more usable form of space travel. Initially this proved to be a great success with many missions flying easily into space and building space stations or launching satellites, but the technology was quite primitive and pilot error or mechanical failure were always a very real worry. The public doubts started when a shuttle exploded at launch and then another didn't make it back through the atmosphere. The public quickly started to ask questions about Franks machine as they considered that it wasn't good enough to deliver the dream and it wasn't long after this outcry before the government pulled the plug on his returnable space experiment and ordered him to do much better next time. The dream had not been completely fulfilled and he knew he would need to improve his plans.

At about this time Michigan announced that he would retire, with sadness at his lack of fulfilling the dream of space travel, he had finally had enough of trying to please everyone and needed some well-earned time to himself. Michigan had spent the last two years of his working life writing his memoirs that when released would prove to be a best seller. Much to Frank's annoyance this detailed book didn't mention any of their time working together. With a heavy heart Michigan passed the mantel of head scientist onto Frank who along with the department inherited the laboratory and all of Michigan's notes, ideas and ongoing projects.

Over the next five years they tentatively worked together with Frank slowly taking the reigns off Michigan and running the department completely as the old man finally retired. Frank was to go on and make a massive discovery within the first year of being alone that would haunt Michigan for the rest of his life. It was something that Michigan had been working on for years and he had been so close but could not get the now seemingly obvious answer. That day Michigan cursed Frank for spotting something so blatantly straightforward that he could never understand how he didn't see it first.

After retiring Michigan became somewhat of a recluse. He had been the most respected member of the scientific community for many years and seemed to have trouble fully resting after his years of public service. Occasionally he would visit the department and enviously look at what they were working on, but he become very slow, tired and any prolonged mental exertion would leave him easily confused. When he visited his old department he never really spent much time with Frank. Frank always felt it was as if he had stolen his job and Michigan had never really want to let it go, despite his advancing years. The truth was that Michigan had never really forgave Frank for finishing his greatest invention and it would give him repeated nightmares to think this younger apprentice had out thought the teacher.

Hans Michigan tragically died only ten years after retiring from the department. On that fateful winters night his last act was to tell Frank the answer to a particularly difficult equation that he had been working on for five years. When he told Frank the answer he felt a warm glow come over him as he finally felt the master had shown the unruly pupil that he didn't quite know everything. Unfortunately for Michigan in his rush to telephone Frank, and tell him the good news, he accidentally left the gas oven on but not lit; as he walked back into the kitchen area of his luxury flat he switched the light on to see where the horrible smell was coming from. The resulting explosion could be seen for miles around and instantly killed probably the greatest scientist the planet had ever seen.

He was duly granted a full state funeral that resulted in many thousands of his admirers lining the streets of the funeral parade to pay their last respects to the one man who had fulfilled more dreams than any other person in history. This incredible public respect for Michigan was Frank's biggest problem and one puzzle that not even his great mind could solve.

Michigan was consistently proving to be an incredibly hard act to follow.

The public had already seen some of Frank's handiwork and were only mildly impressed. The shuttles had quickly become obsolete and his other life changing products had only had marginal successful. The public would still make jokes about his plans for a satellite navigation system combined with robotic legs that would carry you to any destination; this alone was a set back that his reputation had struggled to overcome for many years. He sometimes felt that all the good ideas had been done already and all he could do was improve on his old mentors classic inventions. This was often even more fruitless as many of them were so well thought out that the design would quite easily last forever. All too often, in those early years, he would get his team to paint them another colour and put 'mk II' after the name. He knew this was lazy but he had to give the illusion that the ideas were still flowing out of the department. The government, and more importantly the people, although initially fooled by these actions, quickly noticed laziness in the department. After a short period of time serious questions started to be asked and Frank knew he had to respond in order to get the people back on his side and start to believe he was the person to replace Michigan, the man who had done such a great job of delivering their dreams.

He knew he needed to think bigger and better than ever before. He had an invention that could potentially be a game changer but he wasn't sure if it would work, he knew that if it didn't he would be replaced. After much deliberation and an increased public pressure he decided that he would release details of the invention that he received the call about on that fateful night that Michigan had spoke to him for the last time. This could change everything and propel him to the level of superstar amongst his people.

His only nagging concern was if for some reason it didn't work.

The idea was massive and certainly a game changer, nothing was ever going to be the same again and he would have no choice but to live up to the promises he would make. The consequences of telling everyone about this and then failing were unthinkable, he would have to step down as head of the department or worse he could be fired.

'Fired' the very word that struck fear into every man, woman and child on the planet. Who would want to be fired and have that stigma attached to them? It would be better to commit any other crime than be the only person on the planet without a job.

This sobering thought quickly made up his mind and he picked up the telephone and ordered the press release for the next day.

Chapter 4.

Press release

Frank stood nervously thinking about the upcoming news conference in which he 'Head of Department' would put what's left of his reputation on the line and release details of what he felt was his greatest invention to date. Of course when he said 'his' he actually meant the work of his predecessor and himself after many years of toil and heartbreak. The idea wasn't even complete but it was at the prototype stage and in Frank's eyes that would have to be enough. The ever-increasing pressure on his department for something new was becoming unbearable and the government was beginning to ask questions about his, and the departments, suitability to fulfilling dreams. He did not want to go down in history of the man who didn't only fail, he was also responsible for closing the department.

His colleagues stood around and watched nervously as Frank prepared the final parts of his speech and his presentation for the worlds press. The many hundreds of journalists, that had gathered, knew that this was make or break for Frank. They knew that he could be reprimanded for this or even fired, which until quite recently was deemed as unthinkable. The public sat at home with bated breath as they awaited the appearance of the man who, although recently belittled, still held their futures in his shaking hands.

From behind the partition Frank could hear the familiar noises as the pressroom filled up with reporters from every nation as they jostled for the best seat, setting up cameras and microphones. They all wanted to get the best position from which to record the first speech from the department in nearly thirty years. Frank looked around him for support from his colleagues as the time got nearer and his nerves were on edge of breaking. On many occasions during the last week he had considered the experiments and calculations leading up to this announcement, and convinced himself time and again that he had got everything right. Michigan's final phone call, on that fateful night, had given him the last piece of the jigsaw. It would work and Frank knew in his head that he had got everything correct. The time was now he couldn't wait any longer.

Frank walked slowly onto the stage to muted applause, as the cameras clicked and tapes began to roll, he deftly moved to his seat. He sat and stared out at the many familiar faces from behind a multitude of microphones and tape recorders, and after saying a short prayer in his head, he prepared to speak. He could practically feel Michigan willing him on to make a rash promise to the world, and then fail miserably thus proving his predecessor was better. In his head he knew that this was his time and tried to ignore his thoughts of his mentor. He convinced himself that he could do this and looked to the crowd.

" I have gathered you here today" he commenced through gritted teeth to an eagerly listening crowd, "to discuss and present the greatest invention that this planet has ever seen. It will change our lives forever and finally let us reach for the stars".

The silence in the room was palpable.

"Continuing the work of the great Hans Michigan has been an honour, for me and the department as a whole, and tonight I will show you the labour of his life's work…" Frank looked around the room, there was near silence as he cleared his throat and continued "we have developed a mode of transport that will enable us to travel at nearly eight hundred times the speed of light", there was a collected gasp in the room and cameras started clicking, as he continued "the machine is called the Hyperactive Energy Drive, or HED for short and it will propel us to the stars" as he spoke the curtain came down on a one twenty fourth scale model of the HED, a round of applause followed even though most people in the room had no idea what he was talking about.

"The machine works whereby a life supporting pod will enter one end of the huge funnel at two hundred miles per hour upon entering the drive it will experience massive amounts of electro magnetic force moving the object and its occupants to many other, recently discovered, dimensions. Every time the craft changes through these four other dimensions the craft will increase in speed one thousand times. When it reaches the last section, which is our finest invention and the heart of the HED. The Seminal Magnet Drive and it will increase the speed one hundred thousand times and direct the now tiny craft, and its occupants, yet another dimension that can travel anywhere in the known galaxy in not years but minutes!"

The room fell silent.

The press reporters that were still not in awe of this incredible machine began to ask questions of the invention and how it works.

"How do they land at the other end?" Asked one rather beleaguered reporter who spoke even though he had no idea what Frank was talking about.

"Very good question" replied a now more confident Frank.

"The system works by having the occupants of the other planet building a receiver, to our specification, that will allow the beam to stop. When the beam stops the energy is released and the craft returns to its original size".

Again the room fell into silence as everyone scribbled down notes of the details.

"How will it get there in minutes?" asked a government official who was suddenly interested in what Frank had proposed.

"The compression allows the craft to reach incredible speeds and move through the universe in an up to now undiscovered dimension, which effectively provides a clear line of space between any two fixed points in the universe. As long as we chart the path correctly we can fly to any planet. Providing they are ready."

Frank was now replying with more conviction as he realized that he had discovered the most incredible thing.

"How will we know where to send it?" asked the same reporter.

"I have for many years been studying the universe and looking for stars that support planets, similar to our own, that we can communicate with, give them instructions on what to build and set a date for the craft to arrive", replied a now very confident Frank. His invention was sounding better and better by the moment and he could tell by the reaction in the room that people were buying into his idea.

"These alien beings should complete the building as specified and then we can send our craft and occupants to their planet in a matter of minutes instead of years"

"How will they get back?" asked another reporter as the room began to buzz with chatter.

"They will take with them plans and details of technologies used in the building of the machine. They can then copy it and we will build a super-highway between the two planets. The people of both planets can then commute between the two whenever they wish. Allowing a mutual development of ideas and usage of resources unparalleled in our history", replied Frank.

He scanned the room awaiting the next question and he could tell by the excited vibe that wasn't going to be long in coming.

"Have you any idea where we are going to go?" asked a young lady, who had already caught Franks eye, sat at the front of the auditorium.

"As I have explained", Frank continued, "we have been looking at the universe for the last hundred years trying to confirm where life would be. Our deep space radio telescopes have scanned the universe and we have received on numerous occasions' radio signals from a small planet near a distant small star. Although these signals are primitive we have already worked on communicating with them over many years and soon we will see if we can pop over and visit"

This last statement raised a laugh in the room and the audience was now a fever of activity, news crews were talking on mobiles, conducting interviews live on air and the newspaper reporters were furiously sending e-mails via their computers and phones.

It appeared to Frank that he had hit gold, all his life he had wanted recognition for his work and now he was getting it. By the next day he would be the most talked about man on the planet and he knew that the public would expect him to make this plan work, failure was no longer going to be an option.

The frenzy of activity in the room was not dying down, indeed it seemed to be reaching new highs as everyone became more excited at the prospect of space travel which could not only reach the stars but could also introduce them to new cultures. It was a dream they had chased for so very long and Frank had promised that this dream was now nearly a reality.

"How will we let them know?" shouted a young man over the din in the room that nearly immediately fell silent.

"I am sorry can you repeat the question," replied a now confident Frank.

"How will we let them know we are on the way? And what to build?", repeated the young man, who thought that he had baffled the brilliant professor with what he thought was an elementary fault with the whole thing. It was a brilliant machine and it would send our brave astronauts half way across the universe in minutes, however if the other end didn't know they were coming, how could they build the receiver?

"That is a very good question and one I can more than answer," replied a smiling Frank, who knew what he was going to be saying next.

"We have already tested the machine. We can put a document anywhere we want to within seconds of switching the prototype machine on. Paper based documents, having no physical form, travel instantly as I will now demonstrate."

The whole room watched as Frank turned to the row of scientists behind him and asked them to commence the paper test. Frank stood up and confidently looked to the near silent audience.

"Within the next minute a file of hundred pages will appear in midair and land on this desk in front of me. I can assure you there is no trickery being used and no visual effects are being employed. The prototype HED will send the file through space from my laboratory nearly one hundred miles away and put it in this room before your very eyes in moments" said a suddenly nervous Frank. His nerves had struck at this moment due to his fear that the HED would not work. This would present the members of the public who joked about his achievements with all the material they would need for many more puns at his expense.

There was a fever of activity behind him, including a countdown from five to zero that pre-empted the firing of the HED. In the few moments before the event Frank looked straight into the ensemble of television cameras before him and addressed the world in his moment of glory.

"I want to assure everyone on our planet that this is real. This is the culmination of Michigan's, the departments and my life's work. It is only at the prototype stage but within five years we will have a much larger version capable of transporting man across the stars!" he finished with a flurry and the room fell silent.

The very second that Frank finished his speech a file of papers appeared in the air, before everyone's disbelieving eyes, and slowly fell to the desk.

The HED worked as Frank had said, and the world was stunned.

After letting out a sigh of relief before breaking the silence Frank added,

"We will be sending a file of information to the planet in question within the next year when we have ascertained more data on the people there and the physical details of the planet"

"Do you know anymore about the planet at the moment?" asked a journalist right at the back of the crowd.

Frank looked to his left where the head of the Government was sitting. They exchanged nods and Frank again spoke into the microphones in front of him.

"We know very little of the planet but have ascertained these facts. There star is very small compared to our mighty star, their primitive radio broadcasts would suggest they are less developed than us and lastly and most importantly their planet seems to be, in a physical sense, nearly exactly the same as ours", Frank then sat back looking at the now amazed crowd in front of him.

"Do you have a name for the planet?" shouted a rather over excited person at the front of the room.

Again Frank waited for a nod off the head of government who wilfully agreed;

"Well… they have a name for it, which we have intercepted in their broadcasts"

"They call it Earth."

Chapter 5.

The view behind the fence.

Marshall stood motionless as he stared down at the valley below him. The fence didn't conceal a pit but had been hiding a massive old show. Marshall didn't really understand what he was seeing but he knew he couldn't take his eyes off it.

A huge metal rusting sign that arched above his head between two enormous poles. It was obviously very old and a little battered but it clearly was meant to welcome people to a show of sorts because of how it was written. Marshall quickly thought that it reminded him of the writing outside a circus such was the typeface and the style of the painting. It was a beautiful green and red sign with gold lettering, which clearly said 'Welcome to Earth'.

Marshalls gaze was quickly drawn down into the valley in front of him and he tried desperately to take in the incredible view that had completely taken him by surprise.

The valley was made up of a driveway, which was some twenty metres wide that ran up to a huge satellite dish. Either side of the driveway were lots of buildings of various shapes and sizes that lined the way, some of these buildings were bearing flags of some of the nations of the world. As he studied more he could make out that the buildings were different styles relevant for the different nations, the Japanese flag was on top of a Ming dynasty styled building, the American flag was on top of a huge cowboy styled saloon and right at the top near the satellite dish was a union jack on flying above a miniature houses of parliament. The whole thing looked like a huge exhibition that had either never been finished or had decayed and fallen into disrepair.

It was very obvious to Marshall that this wasn't a 'pit that had gone wrong' as he had been told all his life but was some sort of show that someone, for some reason, didn't want the public to look at anymore.

The view immediately before him was a bank that dropped down some ten metres to the level of the avenue. He could tell that he couldn't possibly go down there tonight as the time was getting on and he knew that his dads game of dominoes would not last that long. He just stood rooted to the spot where he looked at every building in more detail whilst he waited for his dads call. The buildings appeared to be mostly complete but some were not in the best shape as if they had just been left to the elements, and they had certainly been there for a little while but some were definitely better than others.

Marshalls eye was drawn towards the huge satellite dish that was at the end of the roadway. It was pointing straight at him and seemed to be somewhat out of place in this derelict row of buildings. It was certainly in better shape than the rest of the show and to Marshall's way of thinking looked like it had been added later than the buildings as it looked newer and the technology must be more advanced than when these buildings were built. The dish was linked to a row of smaller buildings that were to the left of the road; it was connected by a mass of cables. The buildings were different in design to the rest of the 'show' as they were not decorated in anyway and reminded Marshall of the temporary buildings that adorned his school playground.

Marshalls mind began to wander and he started to form a plan of what he should do next. He had the feeling that he was the first person to ever get through the fence as his footprints on the soft soil were the only ones around and the gap in the fence was tiny, only just big enough for him to get through. He continued to think about what he should do next and who, if anyone, he should tell. He would need to pack his trusted suitcase and he would need to bring some essentials with him:

a torch, some string and perhaps some food preferably chocolate, which was by far his favourite food in the whole world.

He began to fantasise about his discovery and wondered how long it would be before his name was in the newspapers to announce his fame to the world at finding a masterpiece. He could charge people to come in and look, he could run the show as it was meant to be, perhaps he would get rich and then his mum and dad could retire and work with him on the show! However, as quickly as he thought this his cold common sense started to tell him something very different.

What if the people who built this really didn't want it discovered?

What if they would get him and hide him as well?

A cold shiver of fear swept through him as he stood there on the edge of the slope. Indeed, he thought, whoever had built the show had definitely done a good job of covering it up and hiding it. No one he had ever met knew anything other than it was a 'pit that had gone wrong', a statement which never made that much sense to Marshall but he was a child and it was rude to ask an adult if they were wrong.

"Marshall we're goin'!" came the familiar shout from the pubs back door as his dad yelled without looking. Marshall stepped back from the edge and turned for one last glance across his discovery. At this moment Marshall froze, for to the left of the dish in one of the small buildings a light came on.

He quickly tried to remember if the light was on before or had he really just seen it switch on before his very eyes, as quickly as he thought about it the light went out again and a light at a different window came on. Marshall stood staring at the blinking light from his vantage point and in a mixture of fear and excitement he began to think about who was down there.

"Marshall where are you we're goin' to be late!" yelled his dad again this time just a louder. Marshall turned and made his way back to the gap, as he clambered through he glanced back, the lights were now out. He climbed through the fence and back into the pub garden his dad was looking straight at him from the pubs back door. He just waved and beckoned him to hurry up. As Marshall ran across the freshly mowed grass he couldn't help but think that his dad was staring straight at him but he didn't seem to notice him climbing through the fence, this was rather puzzling, as he had always been told not to go near it. As quickly as he thought this he went back to his planning for next week. He was going back behind the fence. He wanted to know what was going on.

The week between visits was the longest week of Marshall's life. He couldn't concentrate on anything as his mind was stuck behind the fence. The questions were endless: What was the show about? Who built it? Why? What? How? These were the questions that were keeping young Marshall awake at night and making him miss most of what his teachers were talking about.

All week he planned for his next visit and packed his trusty brown suitcase accordingly. He had even managed to get hold of his dad's old Polaroid camera, which had three pictures, left in it. His plan was to look around and avoid the cabins at the end. If someone was in there then he didn't want to meet him or her.

The plan was in place and now all he had to do was wait.

The following week was by far the longest of Marshall's short life. He had packed and repacked his trusty old suitcase, which contained, to his mind, everything a young explorer would need to take on this huge challenge. Every night he would go through his plan of what he was going to do when he got back behind the fence. His first step was to make a marker by the gap to ensure he could find his way back. This he would do by putting his 'motorcycling' flag above the opening. Secondly he would descend the slope and make sure he could get back up without too much trouble. This was in order to ensure he could run away from any monsters that may be lurking in the buildings. The buildings may be dark so he had a small red torch, which his parents used for camping holidays and also some birthday candles, and some matches. He also had some paper, a pencil (from his dads plumbing box) and his faithful old friend, a small pottery otter which had no name but he had always seemed to own it.

The days crawled by. Marshall would pace his mother's kitchen and look up at the brown plastic clock which adorned the wall with anguish at its tardiness. School presented its normal long boring summer days presenting information that had been read and re-read for generations, by teachers that saw it as a duty, not a challenge. Whether you understood it or not was irrelevant, the curriculum said it, therefore it was correct. On many occasions during that week he felt the need to tell his friends about his discovery, but he always decided against it. What if his friends went there first? He would no longer be the greatest adventurer of all time.

After what seemed an eternity it was finally Wednesday. School went past in its normal mundane way and Marshalls mum couldn't understand his haste in trying to get home. Every night for as long as his mum could remember Marshall had run out of school and straight onto the park, but not tonight he wanted to get home as soon as possible.

Marshall got eventually got home and after checking and re-checking his case he waited.

After what seemed an eternity his father finally returned home from work and at a snails pace ate his dinner and had a bath. Marshall waited by the door as his dad came down stairs and picked up his car keys.

"We're goin' to the pub!" he shouted to Marshalls mother, as he walked out the door with Marshall in tow, barely waited for a muffled response from upstairs.

'This is it!' thought Marshall as he climbed in his dads' trusty car and they made their way to the pub.

On arrival at the pub Marshall barely waited for the car to stop before he ran around the back of the pub into the fantastic semi-circular garden, which was lined by the fence. He waited patiently at the table for his dad to come out and present him with his evenings nourishment. Within a few minutes his dad emerged from the back door with a bottle of Cola and a bag of crisps.

"That's all your havin' tonight so don't drink it all at once" said his dad with a wink and a smile as he returned back into the pub. Marshall listened for the familiar burst of noise as the door opened and the sudden quiet, as it swung shut.

"This is it!" Marshall spoke to his case out loud as he quickly ate his crisps and wolfed down his pop. With this he climbed down from the table and walked across the field, with a little effort he climbed the slope and crossed the cinder path at the top. As he approached the fence he looked at the gap, it was exactly as he remembered and with a little apprehension he started to climb through.

He was back behind the fence.

He climbed through with no trouble, which was unusual for Marshall, as his mum said he had the ability to trip over a match stick. As soon as he was through he turned and placed his flag on the fence as high as he could reach. He turned around and again his breath was taken away by the incredible view before him.

"No time to sightsee!" he whispered to himself as he walked forward and began to descend the bank onto the main road leading towards the huge satellite dish. He slowly walked along the road trying to take in the views around him. The buildings were in various states of repair and some only seemed to be half finished. He glanced around to check the gap was still there and he could clearly make out his flag hanging limply from the fence.

As he continued to walk towards the dish he felt a little nervous but felt as if he was the only person on the planet. He continued to look around and take in the design of the pavilions around him, they reminded him of the old cricket hut that he walked past everyday on his way to school just on a much bigger scale.

After a short while he arrived at the dish. It sat perfectly still but Marshall could tell by all the machinery that it would have been able to move at some time. The cabins that it was connected to sat lifeless off to his left and to his right he could clearly make out the remains of a cafeteria, which looked like it had never been used. Marshall slowly began to walk towards the cabin where he had seen the lights and, after digging his red torch out of his bag, with a little trepidation opened the door. The room was some kind of control centre that appeared to be in amazingly good condition with many old computers littered around and a few piles of dusty papers on the worktops. Marshall looked around and found an old light switch and with his trembling hand reached out and flicked it. The lights flickered into life in the room and he was immediately bathed in a flood of artificial light. Turning off his torch and placing it back in his case he looked around the room at the old machinery. He was drawn to a machine in the corner, which had an array of flashing lights on top, which kept briefly lighting and disappearing just as quickly.

It was whilst he was looking at the light show before him that he first heard the noise. Every sense in Marshall's body was telling him to run but for some reason he walked towards the closed door at the back of the room. He could definitely hear something but what was it? As he crouched down to listen his brain all to quickly deciphered the noise. It was footsteps and they were getting nearer.

The door handle turned and the door swung open.

Before Marshall stood an old man with white wispy hair who looked straight at him and broke into a smile.

For the second time today Marshall was frozen and his lungs were barren of air.

Chapter 6.

The Professor.

Marshall stood motionless as he looked up at the beaming old man in front of him.

"Well speak then boy!" bellowed the scientist as if he was expecting Marshall to tell him something.

"Who are you?" enquired Marshall, who couldn't believe he was being so gallant.

"I am Professor Ivan B. Stromberg, you don't know me yet but we are going to be friends" piped a very confident and happy old man.

"How do you know that!" retorted a surprised Marshall.

"I know because we are destined to meet and it was only a matter of time before curiosity got the better of someone and they came through that rusty old fence" answered the Professor.

"What is this place?" enquired Marshall who was strangely at ease around this total stranger.

"This is the site of Worlds Fair 1950, or at least it would have been but it was cancelled by the powers that be, or as I prefer to call them the non dreamers!"

"It was cancelled after we had already received the plans to build a hyperlink and as always we started to build exactly to specification. The dish outside is the receiver and we would now be standing in the control pod. The street in front would have been the promenade of countries welcoming them to this planet…"

Marshall stared at the old professor for a while as he listened to his words die off with a tinge of sadness. What was he going on about? What did he mean by 'Them to this planet?' And he couldn't help the fear that was now running through his veins.

"I have to get back to my dad now…" Stuttered Marshall.

"Nonsense!" shouted the professor. "We need to get started straight away on your education!" he continued unabated despite Marshalls hesitance, "Lets develop that young mind that I know will make a difference."

"Anyway your dad will be hours yet, he is still playing dominoes!" said the professor with a nod and a wink to Marshall.

Marshall knew that was the truth and this strange man did seem to know a lot about him,

"How do you know me?" enquired a Marshall who had already started to be interested in the professor and his newfound surroundings.

"Well that would just confuse you at this time" replied the professor "in good time you will understand everything and will be able to assist in the making of the future"

"First you have to understand the past"

The professor beckoned Marshall through to his lab at the back of the building.

There were rows of old looking computers, flashing lights and printers streaming endless prints of what only could be described as numbers in patterns. Marshall thought he had stumbled into the house of a mad person but equally he was intrigued into what the old man had said. He decided that, after checking all the escape routes, he would sit and listen to what the old man had to say.

"In the past we were contacted by others, we know very little about them but what we do know is they are far more advanced than us and want to establish a line of contact between the two planets. They have worked for at least the last two centuries on a machine to get them here at an incredible speed. But the problem has always been at this end, we simply have never had the means to receive the transmission that would establish the link. They have repeatedly been able to send us details of landing sites and ever more extravagant ways of receiving the craft, but alas we have never had a successful landing."

"What do you mean by 'others' mister professor?" asked a confused Marshall.

"Just call me Professor!" laughed the professor before adding "Others, Aliens, people from another planet!"

The professor could see the daunted and frightened look on Marshall's face and quickly moved to ease his fears.

"Don't worry my boy, they look like us! They are exactly the same. They just live on a planet far away," said the professor softly.

"Why don't they just build a spaceship?" asked Marshall trying not to sound like he was stating the obvious.

"Well, this isn't the movies and spaceships are incredibly difficult things to build and power. Then there's the problem of speed. To get anywhere at a decent rate then they would have to travel at the speed of light, and even if they could achieve this it would still take over one hundred years to get here. By which time the people who took off and the ones here on earth would be dead. Instead the others developed a machine which could send items into another dimension that effectively bends space and then they can get here in under two hours." Explained the professor in the simplest terms he could think of.

"How do you know what to build and where?" asked a stunned Marshall.

"Well that's were you need to look into the past" replied the professor who continued, "we have on many occasions received the paperwork and plans for a receiver, and this is the odd bit, they just appear on the Prime Ministers desk in Downing Street."

"What do you mean they just appear?" asked a puzzled Marshall.

"Just that young man, they appear out of thin air, or at least they used too but they stopped when we stopped responding by building the developments they asked for. Of which where you are standing is the last development which was scrapped half way through because the government stopped believing it was possible and simply pulled the plug on all the hard work that had gone before it."

"The annoying thing was we were so close, I know we were so close for one reason and for one reason have I kept working and trying to establish the link. And that is Galaxy…"

"What is Galaxy?" retorted a stunned Marshall.

"Galaxy is a capsule!" beamed an excited Old Man as he opened a wall unit to reveal a silver bullet shaped container with 'Galaxy 1' written on the side.

"They sent it with the very last transmission before the blasted council turned off the power!" shouted the professor. "They went and powered three villages with the electric instead. No dreamers in the council, my boy, just bloody minded beauricrats!"

The professor slowly lifted down the silver container and opened the locks on the door. He slowly and carefully lifted out a transcript which when he opened it revealed a map of the night sky.

"This, young man, is a map of the Martian sky! Some of the stars we can see on an evening but many others on here are not visible from Earth. This small red arrow in the middle is the approximate position of Earth". The professor continued to show Marshall the map and explain all the stars and relativity to Earth.

Marshall looked around the room at the machines and one screen in particular which was labelled rather crudely as 'sender'. The professor caught his stare and explained some more.

"The tracker shows us exactly where the beam is coming from and allows us the luxury of a very crude if not effective link between the planets. This allowed them to talk to us and give us updates on what was happening up there and also they told us things that have helped us to develop our technology"

"The only problem was that the governments of the world decided that some of what they gave us was better for Military usage and not for exploring the stars, once the others caught wind of this the transmissions stopped."

"The link is still open on the tracker but they never answer us. I try every day to establish contact but its as though they are angry at their technology being misused by our primitive and war happy civilization."

Marshall was stunned and a little confused. He croaked into life as the professor stared at him.

"How did you know I would come here?" he asked

"Well" said the professor clearing his throat, "the last transmission I received here in 1952 informed me that they were working on better technologies and would contact me regarding the future links sometime in the next twenty years. You are the first person to get down here after the fence was constructed so it must be you"

"It was easy," replied Marshall " there's a great big hole in the fence I just squeezed through and saw everything! Anyone could have done it"

"Well there lies the answer my boy," stated the smiling professor.

"The fence was built to an alien design that would hide me away down here and would stop people asking questions. It is also completely impenetrable to anyone who isn't allowed in"

Marshall looked at the mad man in front of him as he continued.

"You see young Marshall you are allowed in, you are the only person to walk through that fence in twenty-five years even though it is plain view of everyone!" explained the professor as he pointed out the window to the outer fence.

"Have you never noticed that no one talks about it?" the professor asked Marshall as he shook his head.

"My dad said it was a pit gone wrong," replied a now more comfortable Marshall.

"My boy! How can a pit go wrong?" laughed the professor.

"They all say that because they cant understand the fence. It tells them to think like that so they stay away, they don't ask about things they don't understand."

"Its human nature. They are blind to the obvious the pub is a huge arrow pointing this way but no one has ever bothered to look."

"Except you" smiled the professor as he pointed straight at Marshall.

Marshall started to realize that he was the only person who ever looked at the fence. He could remember the children playing but not one mentioned the fence it seemed like everyone was oblivious to it. Only he had found a gap but the more he thought about it the more obvious the gap was. The whole thing is massive but no one looks. His tiny mind was racing now and he wasn't scared but just really curious.

"What about planes?" asked Marshall, after what seemed an eternity.

"Good boy! Now you are waking up! Planes don't see us because people don't look; it's a classic bit of diversion. There is nothing around here except old pits and older houses, nothing of any interest so people just don't look even though it is in plain sight. Their minds are closed, they can see no further than what they are told, they believe everything they are told and are happy that way."

"But you are different, you saw the fence on the first visit to the pub, you dreamt of what was here and then you came looking for more and here we are. You and mankind can achieve anything if they just opened their minds and looked at what we have already got." The professor could make out the inquisitive look on Marshalls face and felt the need to explain more.

"Tell me Marshall can you fly?" asked the professor.

"No I can't!" replied Marshall.

"Why" asked the professor smiling,

"Because I don't have wings or an engine and I am too heavy" stated a confident Marshall.

"Who told you that?" laughed the professor.

"Its common knowledge" stated a now confident Marshall, who had listened to everything he had been taught at school.

"Well its wrong! Bees cannot fly, the physics and aerodynamics are all wrong! But no one bothered to tell them so they just carry on flying around without a care in the world" answered a smiling professor.

"So are you saying I can fly?" replied an excited Marshall.

"No you can't. I just used that as an example. But it proves a point doesn't it" laughed the professor.

"What does it prove?" questioned a puzzled Marshall

"We believe what we are told to believe, the government knows we have had contact with aliens. Over the years various Presidents, scientists, Kings and Queens have had contact but the public just get told what to believe. UFO's and fanciful alien stories are a hoax developed by the governments to keep us looking up and not sideways. I mean how daft are people to believe that aliens would fly half way across the universe, in some fanciful machine that defies gravity, and then upon arriving in Bognor Regis flash the lights three times and then fly off without so much as saying a word!" the professor knew he was ranting on a little but Marshall appeared to be lapping up the information.

"Its not like we are the most interesting people is it?" shouted the professor.

"They would come here and invade if they existed. I know the bloke who invented the UFO his name is Arthur Blythe and he is from Leicester. Now I know that's a distance from here but its not exactly another universe is it?"

"Every government and high ranking official for the last two hundred years has known about these projects but not told the people. They didn't need to; they just released new technologies upon the public and said some clever bloke had invented it! It makes our life easier and because we're happier we don't ask questions. If we don't ask questions and then over many generations people stop asking questions all together."

"They built UFO's to stop people looking! Rather predictably in true human fashion everyone bought it! Roswell was a weather balloon, no one has ever been abducted and we have never been near the moon! We have trouble keeping planes in the air so I have no idea how the public bought that one!" Ranted the professor.

"What else?" asked Marshall who was suddenly fascinated by the views of this mad scientist.

"Well my boy, over the coming years I will tell you everything but for now let me tell you that everything that mankind thinks they invented they really didn't!" the professor replied cryptically.

"Marshall, you will one day reveal all. But first we have many things to learn!" said a very excited old man.

"And another thing… the earth is flat"

"Is it?" replied a startled Marshall.

"No it's round, but for a minute there you believed me!" replied a smiling professor.

The Bomb.

It was the middle 1944 and the President was beside himself with worry.

Here he was in the midst of the biggest world war to ever grip the planet, he was also flying blindly into a financial recession and his people, and more importantly his investors, were not at all happy.

He knew that War is an economic and political time bomb that few politicians ever survive. The President also knew that his countries initial support and inclusion in World War Two had given his workforce a much-needed boost but over the time had become a drain on all their resources. The most important thing to his beleaguered people was the massive loss of young men during this mainly European conflict, which with the inclusion of the Eastern countries had rapidly turned into an all out World War. The war in the east was costing many millions of dollars and many thousands of men were laying down their lives for, in the public's opinion, no reason. That was until Pearl Harbour when every American demanded action to stop these nations before they attacked the mainland again.

The President knew that he needed solutions to end this war and fast. The voting public was rapidly running out of patience and he knew that this would be reflected in the opinion polls and more importantly at the polling stations in the next few years.

On top all these pressing problems he had received another annoying communication from London with yet another fanciful plan of a landing post for the 'Others' to land on.

He was somewhat fed up with the plans that kept arriving and had developed a personal disbelief in the projects, even though they had heralded some of the greatest 'discoveries' of our time. These landing posts were always so grand, so expensive and so prone to failure that he had trouble even thinking of the cost, but he was sure of one thing, it would contain many zeroes and take some getting past congress in these war-torn years.

It only took two days, from putting the plans to congress, before he was sat in his office with a blank cheque to build the receiver and instructions that if it was to go wrong that America wanted sole rights to any 'discoveries' that would be revealed, whatever they may be.

The scheme for the receiver was the most bizarre contraption to date. This steel structure, which was built just off shore, would enable the spacecraft to float down and use the seawater to cool the outer shell. Hopefully this would stop the massive amounts of heat that were being generated by the 'flight' and allow the craft to land slide up the ramp and stop safely on the shore.

A site had already been picked just off the shore of a magnificent shingle beach in the county of Suffolk in England.

During the war years this tiny fishing hamlet was to be evacuated in order to complete military 'tests' and upon its seclusion from war torn Britain the metallic structure was quickly completed over the following twelve months.

On the fateful day in September 1941 the military sat at an adjoining beach, in a viewing tower, as the bright flaming craft appeared over the North Sea. As the craft coasted onto the water it destroyed the steel landing stage in a fountain of sparks and explosions. The main hull of the craft ripped open dropping fuel onto the pitch-black nighttime sea. The sparks rained down igniting the fuel and turning the sea into a blazing carpet of fire. The disabled craft hit the shingle beach spraying millions of pebbles all around before sliding up the beach destroying the disused fishing vessels in its wake. Finally the vessel came to rest after smashing through the front doors of the local tavern before exploding and completely destroying the building, along with the spacecraft and the poor travellers who were trapped within.

The ensuing explosion could be seen for many miles around and in the aftermath the British public were told they were testing new kind of bomb and the area wasn't going to be safe for a number of years. When the fire had finally been extinguished the American secret service started to sift through the remains of the pub and eventually found a case full of plans and diagrams amongst the burnt embers.

The paperwork arrived back in the United States of America approximately two weeks after the magnificent failure in Suffolk. It was marked as confidential and, much to all the other allied countries distaste was only for the Americans. The President and his advisers slowly opened the envelopes and out fell masses of plans, pages of instructions and mathematical jargon. The President didn't care for all these papers, as all he wanted was the letter that he eventually found sealed in the larger envelope. He quickly unfolded the letter and read with haste:

'If you are reading this letter then we are sorry for our failure on this occasion. We have lost many good men on this terrible day, but will continue to strive to link with you soon. Please destroy all plans of this receiver, as it is a faulty and an obviously useless design.

As a sign of our faith in you and your continued patience please accept our apologies and these plans for a compact Super Nuclear Reactor of which we have used successfully for many years. If you build one you will produce enough free electric to power your entire planet for eternity.

Many thanks.

Frank Farley II

Ps. Make sure you build it exactly to our specification otherwise there is a very great danger that you will build a very powerful and compact bomb which will cause devastation.'

"A bomb?" questioned a puzzled President turning to his advisors.

He quickly passed the plans to his scientists, who excitedly greeted the injection of new ideas with open arms, as he pushed passed them and into his private office where he immediately picked up the telephone. The best and most creative minds on the planet wondered at this new promise of eternal free power for all, and the new technology contained in the super powerful and reliable reactor plans. They excitedly commenced work on deciphering the codes immediately and planning prototypes.

Their excitement at these great discoveries for mankind was rapidly cut short when the President eventually emerged from his office and shouted out a few blunt words that would change everything on Earth forever.

"Forget the free power, that's a mugs game!" he shouted at the banks of scientists as they stopped reading the information and looked towards him in disbelief.

"I want us to be the most feared and respected country on this planet and end this bloody war!"

"Build me a bomb!"

His order rang around the room like a death knoll and signalled the beginning of the most fruitless and pointless era in mankind's chequered, war-torn and hateful history.

The events that ensued over the following year destroyed any faith man could ever have in the politicians as the ensuing bomb proved to be the most devastating development to ever be used in anger. Many thousands of people died at the detonation and development of what was supposed to be a useful and peaceful design that would improve life for everyone of earth. The others looked down from the heavens and wept in disbelief as a few men were allowed to turn one of their greatest gifts into a weapon that had been unimagined anywhere else in the universe.

The others declared that the day the first atomic weapon was used would always be a day of remembrance for the innocent lives that would be affected by their mis-used design for many generations. The day also signalled the time that the others decided that there would be no further contact with Earth. The people of earth could not be trusted and the others had watched for years as mankind had developed into a race that could not control itself. It also appeared to excel in allowing a few bad people to inflict needless and hateful crimes on its own helpless, innocent people.

The Cold War that stretched over the next forty years not only puzzled Frank and his people but it angered them at the incredible narrow mindedness of man as they spent ever more time on researching and developing bigger and better weapons that could destroy their own planet many times over. They could not believe the sheer hatred of the people of the little blue green planet, of which they had desperately tried to not only help but also become part of for over two hundred years.

The devastated people of his planet ordered that Frank must never contact the Earth again. Frank suffered a breakdown, as it was his decision to include that technology on that doomed flight. He blamed himself for mankind's ridiculous and pointless arms race. Every night in his dreams he would hear the screams of the innocent souls as they suffered at the hands of mans destruction. The department was temporarily closed whilst he recovered.

The communication device that had been used for decades to contact Earth was switched off and removed on that very sad day.

The people of Earth never knew it but their best friend had once again become a stranger.

Chapter 7.

Questions, questions, questions…

Marshall stood staring at the Professor as he wandered around the room explaining all the various machines and their uses. He explained the whole laboratory at a break-neck speed that achieved little more than confused Marshall even more as it seemed like he was talking in a foreign language. Marshall stood politely listening to the rambling old man before he finally built up enough courage to start a rather curt and shy conversation.

"How does it work?" enquired a rather bemused Marshall,

"That is a very good question!" replied a happy Professor, "and one that I cannot completely answer, the technology is far and above what we understand here on earth, but they use materials which we have readily available, which is a little odd because to our knowledge they have never been here" continued the Professor looking increasingly puzzled, as if he was pondering a question which had disturbed him for a millennia.

"Perhaps they have…" Marshall responded.

"Well they said back in '32 that they hadn't, but they had had a good look around with their powerful observation telescopes. Amazing if you ask me, they could look from space into our own backyards and decide where and how to build these machines", the Professor looked saddened and a little jealous that he hadn't got that sort of technology to play with.

"Where are you from?" asked Marshall

"Ah good boy your brains slowly waking up" said a happier professor before adding, "I was brought up in a small town in Derbyshire and always loved science. When I was old enough I took my things and went to university where I excelled in all things scientific. I was soon noticed by the contemparies of my day and was offered a job with Thomas Edison, but a friend of mine Nikola Tesla told me that he would steal my ideas so instead I went to work at Teslas new company in America. After that company failed I went to work for the American Government and was scientific adviser on the Worlds Fairs of 1933 and 1936. That is when I first had contact with the others and that bought me all the way to this point. Anyway! Enough of the past we must look at the future!".

"What about your family?"

"I never had time really, always been busy building things. I did have a wife once but she's gone now and my parents were killed in the war. My life Marshall has been dedicated to bettering mankind. Building a better future was my dream when I left university and it is still my dream now after all these years. The link would have opened the stars for us and how I would have loved to see them. There's a whole universe out there and one day I will get us there!"

The professor was certainly passionate about the others and his passion was infectious as Marshall was getting more excited with every sentence. He had always dreamed of changing the world but this professor really seemed to know how to do it.

"These machines they told you to build?" responded a suddenly interested Marshall.

"Oh yes, my boy, this was the last of a long line of ever more extravagant failures dating back over hundreds of years and each producing a more determined attempt next time!" the professor again looked saddened that the efforts never produced a true tangible result.

"When and where?" asked Marshall who had made himself comfortable next to a rather odd looking machine that kept producing noises like a trapped cat.

"Now where shall I begin" pondered the professor, "ah I know! World Fairs! Every World Fair since they began way back in Victorian days at the Crystal Palace. The story goes that the Prince received the plans and built the first receiver in only nine months, didn't work! But they moved it and eventually it did sort of operate, well it burnt to the ground but at least they tried. Since then every now and then we receive a message from the others telling us what to build, where to build it and most importantly when they would attempt to 'land'", pausing for breath the professor continued.

"Well I say 'land', what they actually do is transmit a spaceship through space and time to wherever the receiver is. This decodes the transmission and, in theory, they materialize before our very eyes"

"Unfortunately there has always been a problem somewhere along the line and many men have been lost due to our joint technological failures"

"What was the worst?" asked an intently interested Marshall

"1933 Worlds Fair!" shouted the professor, making Marshall jump.

"Probably the biggest and most exotic of all the Fairs of the time. They even sent plans of exhibits and houses to build but the most interesting part was the Skyride. It was an enormous cable car set between two massive towers with viewing platforms. To the general public it was a magnificent example of mans ability to build incredible structures, to us in the 'loop' it was a huge receiver that would allow the others to send data and a spaceship all the way across the stars."

"But that wasn't all, so confident were the others of success that it would also allow a return journey. The cable cars were actually airtight spaceships that when the time was right were to be loaded with men and sent all the way to their planet."

"What went wrong?" asked Marshall.

"We don't know. We did exactly as we were told. We built it exactly to specification and in the correct place. We were told to open the show when the light from the star Sirius lined up with our receiver the energy from this would power the transmitter and within minutes we could open the gateway to the stars"

"Obviously it didn't go to plan, we got a call from Downing Street within an hour of the day saying that there was a delay at their end and the transmission would be two years late!"

"So what did you do?" asked a startled Marshall,

"Well we kept the exhibition open for two years instead of one, and to be honest it was a massive success there were many things that the public wanted to see, robots, houses of the future, transport and such like. The public lapped it up but when the time for transmission arrived the show was shut by the government for safety reasons and we prepared to receive the transmission."

"The others weren't happy about this as they wanted to arrive for all of mankind not just for a select few. And they had also found out a lie that had been happening for years." Added the professor.

"They found out that the inventions they had been sending us, to help mankind progress, had not only been kept secret but had been used to make war machines and weapons. They were not happy about this and threatened that if it continued the link would never happen. The government assured them that this wouldn't happen again but of course it did."

"Anyway, the night arrived and we powered up our transmitter and prepared to launch the countdown progressed and at exactly one in the morning of Christmas day 1935 we launched, well I say launched, the pod went down the cable towards the other tower at twenty three miles per hour and disappeared, at exactly the same moment a ball of flame appeared coming the other way, straight at us, which was their pod arriving after flying over the universe!"

"What next!" asked a rather excited Marshall.

"We managed to stop the pod and after fighting the ensuing fire we opened the doors, only to find everyone inside had been incinerated. All that was left was box of files showing plans for various flying machines and computers. The military grabbed those before we could look properly but there was some good stuff in there!", explained the professor.

"What about our pod!" asked the excited Marshall.

"It made it complete and not on fire! We sent our pod half way across the universe and it arrived on their doorstep complete and full of lovely earth air!"

"What about the people?" asked Marshall.

The professor looked at him and the tears welled in his eyes.

"They were gone. Not a trace of them anywhere. We nor the others have ever figured it out as to where they went or what happened to them…" his voice cracked a little as he added, "my wife was on that ship, she had to go, I asked her not to but she was adamant that she wanted to reach across the stars. Also on board were two other professors who were friends of mine and my mentor senior professor Mark Hallimore, one of the most brilliant men to ever grace this good earth."

"I am sorry for your loss but I have never heard of him!" said Marshall.

"He taught Einstein Physics and discovered a small theory, of which someone else took credit." Replied the professor.

"We didn't hear anything from them for a while after that, in fact where you are stood is the last attempt before they discovered the evil truth behind men"

"What's that?" asked a rather naïve Marshall.

"All they did with all those wonderful plans was build ever more elaborate weapons, until they noticed what was happening and then they stopped helping us and simply stopped talking to us. Mankind was given all it needed to know for free energy, which could be transmitted through the airwaves and what did we do with it? We built the nuclear bomb. Probably the most devastating weapon ever to be unleashed in the universe."

"Of course they saw it and they saw what happened at the end of World War two, they saw what we did to two hundred thousand innocent individuals and then they saw the ridiculous waste of time and money that has followed since. The Cold War should have been named 'Mans Greatest Folly'. We were given gifts, which would let us reach out and be not just a planet, but populate a Galaxy, but no, we looked at other men and tried to wipe them out. The others saw what effectively they had started and stopped talking, sending plans, trying and dreaming of helping man. We built the most effective weapon of all, the power to stop dreams"

The Professor looked sad and drained.

"You had better go Marshall, yours dads just finishing his drink."

"How do you know that!" replied a startled Marshall.

"He's on this screen here via wireless video connection" said the Professor.

"The what?" said Marshall whilst doing a good impression of a startled rabbit.

"Don't worry its not been invented yet" the Professor replied smiling.

Chapter 8.

The Presidents Dream.

It had been a winter of turmoil after the election of the youngest president in the history of the country. There had been demonstrations, roadblocks, riots and mass hysteria regarding the ongoing and devastating recession, which had gripped the public in its cold grip and refused to let go. Many large companies were in trouble and the young president was being tested of his abilities, and moreover his promises, to get this once great country moving again.

Sitting in the oval office he surveyed the mass of paperwork on his desk that had become his life. Cutbacks was his middle name to many voters, which had caused him some concern, he didn't like this moniker as he had always wanted to be known as 'the great leader' or 'the saviour', 'President Cuts' just didn't ring the same. In his heart he wanted, and needed to, do something to change the fortunes of his great and powerful country. He knew that they had become somewhat of a laughing stock amongst the powerful nations, as the one thing they couldn't control was their economy. He knew he had to do something different that would ignite the people of his country to rise up and fight the aggressive grip of this recession that had decimated their ability to win.

His life was controlled by his need to do something that would change the fortunes of the economy and change the sorry path that his once great country had now taken. The advice he was receiving from his party was basically the same tried and tested strategies that had failed a hundred times before. He felt absolutely useless as he ran out of ideas and his advisers and party members were even worse. There was absolutely nowhere to turn when in a moment of unguarded inspiration he had an epiphany.

'Worlds Fair'. The idea flashed into his head, shining like a powerful torch in a darkened room. He couldn't understand where the idea had come from but he was now confident that he had finally hit on something, which would inspire the public to lift out of this hated recession.

Why hadn't he thought of this earlier? Not a typical run of the mill exhibition or expo, this would be bigger and better than any of the fairs of old. He could visualize the whole thing in his head. It wouldn't just be another expo but would hark back to the days of massive Worlds Fairs that would inspire mankind to dream again. They would fire the imagination of people to get up and fight off the chains of depression that had weighed them down for so many years. He knew that he could get his country to dream again just like our recent ancestors had done. His World's Fair would have every person in the world being shown the future and how great it was going to be, with his country right at the centre of it. They would show the most extreme designs from every inventor, company or crankcase in the world. The only criteria would be is that these inventions would have to change something and develop a worldwide dream. He would lead this fantastic show and he could show his plans for a whole new world that he could lead. This would demonstrate to the public that there were still dreams that he and his government could show them and hopefully fulfil. This was his chance to show the world, and more importantly his country, that there were inventions out there that would not only look good but could make a tangible difference to everyone.

The image of what he wanted was in his head like a photograph and he could never remember having such a stark realization of what he wanted to do. Later in the day, when he was finally allowed to rest from the hustle of politics, he slouched back on his bed and allowed himself to dream a little.

In his mind he could picture the entire Worlds Fair like an architectural plan. This plan he could then turn it into a three-dimensional visualization of the entire fair that he could dream of walking through. He could allow his mind to show him into every pavilion, exhibition and amusement. Most importantly he could even picture the look on people's faces... smiles, loads and loads of lovely smiles. He knew that all his country needed, to escape this downturn, was smiles and dreams. He also knew that he had to sort this out for his people and for the first time since becoming President his mind was set on exactly what to do.

The very next day a board of all the departments was called to the White House for what was billed as an 'Electoral winning meeting'.

As the room filled with the various heads of department, some of which were fresh off the plane, the President couldn't remember being so confident in front of these powerful and at times dominating people. He stood at the head of the table and looked down at his eagerly listening colleagues.

"We are going to build a Worlds Fair" started a confident and strident President,

"We are going to build the biggest and best Worlds Fair that has ever been constructed," he continued ignoring the already outstretched arms of some parties, "it will bring the people of Earth together on our glorious shores and we will show them that the United States of America is the world leader, we will demonstrate the best things we have to offer and start to rebuild the dream of a better future for everyone."

"I want the people of this planet to lift themselves out of this horrific recession in the same way that our fore-fathers did. This was not by demanding answers from others but by seeing what was available and building a dream. This will only be completed by getting off our collective backsides, to stop talking about it and start actually building towards a better future."

The room had a strange silence to it and it was clear that everyone was in shock. There were some strange, puzzled looks being glanced between the leaders of industry, before someone finally had the courage to speak up;

"How are we going to build a huge fair when we have no money?" asked the obviously shaken Minister of Finance, after quickly doing some maths in his head.

"I was expecting you to ask me that, as money is always our biggest problem and I will show you the answer" replied a confident President before adding, "this country is suspending all Military action, Policing of foreign shores, all weapon development and construction costs. This alone will save us billions of dollars a year. Instead of wasting this money we will direct at doing something good. Instead of the wasteful and pointless cost of war in far flung countries which mean nothing to our people and feed the opposition with propaganda we will build a Worlds Fair of immense proportion".

"We are mostly self sufficient, as a country, in energy and resources. If we need extra workers then we will employ previously unemployed people and build their lives and families as well. This will have a two fold effect, firstly by giving these people a wage and secondly it will give them a purpose".

The President was now feeling unstoppable and continued to elaborate on his visual plan with the many slides and drawings he had personally prepared for the meeting. He had also spoke to some private companies and calculated how all the services could combine and help to build the fair. This would be achieved by relocating staff and resources to one common objective.

"We will build the fair to open in May 2020. It will be the biggest and best fair ever constructed and there will be an open invitation to every nation in the world to attend and show their latest technologies, developments and most importantly dreams."

He stopped and looked at the now more than shell shocked audience.

Their faces all looked so scared of his proposals and he waited for the inevitable feedback of doubt and questions. He didn't have very long to wait before someone spoke.

"I think this could be a great idea" said a young scientist who was stood at the back of the room.

Everyone turned to see a young man who looked the epitome of how a crazed scientist should look. His balding head was surrounded by an unruly mop of hair and his smile beamed out from an unshaven and bespectacled face. He stepped forward, towards the opposite end of the table, and his aura immediately grabbed the limelight.

"It is a great idea because it is exactly what mankind needs. We need a dream a belief and something to aim at and what could be a better way of doing that than inviting everyone to look and feel the future." He spoke out with an un-erring confidence that left most of the room silent.

This degree of enthusiasm immediately grabbed the President's attention and he beckoned him forward to say more. With a renewed aplomb the young scientist continued:

"I know the fairs of old developed a belief in the people that there was more to come and kept the peoples heads up in the dark times. The people knew there was something to aim for, something to achieve and the World would be a better place" he turned to the room and continued "the Worlds Fairs developed a generation of people who believed we were working for them, to make their lives better through technology". He turned back around and suddenly saddened he addressed the President.

"Your predecessors have continually let them down and spoon-fed them bad news about the economy, the environment and so forth. Now you and your government have the chance to put this right and stand tall in a history littered with injustice."

"Mankind is capable of many great things as we have proved time and again over the centuries. It is time to stop thinking like Neanderthals, by building weapons and committing acts of war and start thinking like Gods. We have the ideas and the capability to build a better and more secure future. This depression could be remembered as a starting point where man put down his weapons and let science take us to the next level. My mentor always knew that one day someone would open their mind and understand. All the people in this room are capable of starting this change."

"What you could be part of would be historic for all the right reasons."

"Science and all the many departments of this Country could work with you all to develop a memorable event which will attract millions of people and dazzle every man, woman and child on this planet via television and the Internet. We could help them to dream again and most importantly believe in their leaders to take them to a better future for themselves and their children. You could be the heroes that achieve this."

"You people are the key to writing the future and taking mankind out of the dark ages and propelling him to the stars!" The young scientist finished with a flourish and turned to look at the President.

The President thought for a moment and looked at the young man in front of him. He quickly realized that he didn't only not know who this person was, he also had no idea where he had come from or who he worked for.

"Where and for whom do you work?" asked the President.

"I work for the Stromberg Institute in Chicago, as the Scientific Director. We work directly for your government to advise on anything from genetically modified foods in schools to space exploration. There are some brilliant and talented people in the Institute who could, and will, help you to build this dream." replied the confident scientist.

"What's your name?" asked a very inquisitive President.

"Sir, you can call me Marshall." replied a smiling scientist.

Chapter 9.

Marshall grows up.

For Marshall life was good. The long hazy days of his childhood passed by mostly without a worry. Every time Marshall went to school he made sure he learnt something new, he knew he needed every morsel of knowledge to help him through life. It also gave him something new to talk to the Professor about on his weekly visits. He was a smart, articulate child but he rarely poked his head above the parapet, preferring to stay below the radar and taking a back seat when in one of the team situations that his school seemed to love so much.

Marshall excelled in a few subjects particularly maths and physics, they were his personal favourites, but there were hardly any subjects that he couldn't turn his hand to if required. The problem mainly lay in Marshall himself. He knew that there was another place; a superior race and he knew that half the things he was taught in history lessons were simply fabrications invented by men to cover-up the truth of what was really going on.

For a while during his first years at school he would challenge the teachers to explain more, while always being careful not to reveal his beliefs for fear of ridicule. He would often listen intently and in his mind the professor would be answering the teacher as he spoke:

'The Eiffel tower is a piece of art in Paris" the teacher would preach.

In Marshall's mind the Professor would reply:

"No, it's just a badly built receiver no more than iron junk!"

"The Statue of Liberty was a gift from France to America…"

"I think you will find it was a basic telecommunications mast built to receive interstellar communications, built incorrectly by the French. Again"

"The Americans developed the Nuclear weapon…"

"NO! They used a fantastic invention which would have given all mankind free electricity and turned it into a devastating weapon of war which would threaten every man, woman and child on the planet"

"Einstein's theory of relativity…"

"Free information blasted across space, claimed by a hobo!"

"Nikola Tesla was a mad scientist that believed electricity could be beamed free around the world…"

"In fact Nikola Tesla was a genius. He was part of one of the teams that deciphered the information sent to us. What he discovered was not science fiction, it was fact. It was a fact that the others had not even thought of."

'He developed something not even the others had thought of!' he would hear the professor shouting this in disbelief.

"Amongst many other great inventions Nikola Tesla invented a way of transmitting electricity through the air to any device on the planet. He used the earth as a transmitter and you just plugged in!"

"The invention worked, crudely, but it worked! Not only that but the others took the invention back off him and developed it. They tried to tell us but as usual we got it all wrong! The power companies got heed of the situation and manufactured a story to dismiss the poor man and ridicule him."

The others were so impressed by Tesla that they started to talk to him directly. Over many years he invented many things on his own that the others took and used.

He even developed a machine, which revealed how the others were transmitting to earth by intercepting the radio signals.

The others could see what mankind couldn't, and that was the simple fact that Tesla was simply a genius. He could visualise and develop machines in his head, he could ponder many problems at the same time and he knew how to build dreams. The others tried in vain to get Tesla to build them a receiver but as he got older his brilliant mind began to fail and they never got to directly work with him. They would often hold a moment's thought for this great man and sit in disbelief at mankind's inability to respect brilliance.

As Marshall daydreamed in class during the day he worked incredibly hard at night. Many nights he would not sleep until the early hours as he pawed through endless books and research papers that the Professor had sent him. He would spend those hazy summer nights at the pub, not playing football with the other children, but behind the fence in the laboratory wiring up machines and asking endless questions to test the Professors knowledge.

He had indeed bought the Professor back to life with his enthusiasm and his never-ending drive for answers. Marshall was very rapidly becoming a very capable scientist and was having ideas that would often stun the Professor with their complexity.

Marshall challenged every idea that was currently accepted as the norm. Every theory and equation would be punished, tested and re-tested until Marshall could determine once and for all that they were correct. The Professor would sit back and smile, as Marshall got older, and he watched his student develop into one of the greatest minds on the planet.

All the time that this was happening they were transmitting a message to the stars, asking for help and contact. The contact would come eventually but not before the others could trust us again, and that would take a while after the Cold War had ended.

Apart from his excursions behind the fence Marshall led a relatively normal upbringing. He would attend school, play with his friends, try to be good at football and sit at night staring at the stars. The only difference between Marshall and other children his age was that when he stared at the stars he knew there were others up there in the distant galaxies. He also knew that they could watch us and he wouldn't know how much they were watching until a few years later when he had his first actual contact.

One night he was sat looking out the window when a UFO flew past. He knew it wasn't real, but his friends were ecstatic and called the local press who promptly interviewed them all. Of course when they spoke to Marshall he told them outright that it was a fake, the reasons he gave were exactly what the Professor had told him all those years previously. The reporter didn't write anything down and wasn't over favourable with Marshall either, openly calling him a 'weird kid'. The other kids wouldn't go out at night for a while, for fear of being abducted, Marshall would go out walking every night and stand looking at the skies.

One day he knew in his heart that he would reach for the stars, not only that he would hopefully take mankind with him. He would show mankind how to fly to the stars to be a better race and more importantly he would stop them fighting. A tall order for anyone but for this boy of fourteen years it would be a mountain to climb, but he knew with the Professors' guidance he could achieve anything.

Marshalls Mum and Dad believed in him to. They knew he was bright and some of the stories he would tell would seem fanciful and unbelievable. He would tell them of his thoughts on many subjects, from UFO's to space travel. He would explain everything he knew and no page would be left unturned with them.

They were his best friends.

They never knew the Professor but he sure wished he could have introduced them. The only thing stopping this was the fence. The Professor would not come out of the base and no way could he get his parents through that fence.

" The pit behind there is dangerous and I don't want to see you trying to get through," said his Dad, when Marshall approached the subject one day.

" I don't want you going through there," said his worried Mum, *" there might be a funny man behind there who will take you away…"*

Marshall smiled at his Mum's comments, yes, there was a *'funny man'* behind the fence and, yes, he was going to *'take him away'*.

Far away beyond the stars.

It was another familiar Wednesday night, just a week after Marshalls fifteenth birthday, when the receiver finally sparked into life. Marshall was drinking a nice cup of tea and sharing his favourite malted milk biscuits with the Professor. They had just discussed the theory of relativity and the Professor had explained to him how it was wrong and how Teslas' theory was correct. At first neither of them noticed the red light flashing on top of receiver, but when they finally did the only sound to break the silence was the Professors cup as it smashed to the floor.

They both slowly walked over to the kiosk and with the seemingly slow motion of old hands the Professor reached forward and flicked a bright orange switch. With this the screen in front of them sparked into life and the image of a well-dressed middle-aged man appeared before them.

"Hello Ivan. How are you?" spoke a smiling Frank Farley.

Marshall could only stare in awe and think of the first time he heard that name, all those many years ago when he was only a small boy.

"I am fine Frank. It has been too long old friend, but I must say you are looking well for two hundred and ten years old!" replied a smiling professor.

"It has been too long", said Frank.

"What do you want us to do?" asked an anxious professor.

"Well old friend. Now you have finally found a capable assistant", Frank said motioning towards Marshall, "We are actually prepared to give Earth one last chance. We really want to link and feel we together can benefit from each others vast knowledge and ability"

"We will now have regular contact with you two and will send plans to build the next receiver. You will recognise the design Ivan. We know this works as long as it is built in exactly the right place and perfectly to our design," continued Frank as he slowly rotated his gaze towards Marshall.

"You, Marshall, are the future. We believe in you and your ability. Listen to Ivan he will guide you on what to do. Keep the faith in us and the rewards for you and mankind will be enormous. The Cold War will end soon and all but a few of your small-minded politicians will have forgotten about us. You alone will introduce us to Earth" with that final word the transmission faded and Frank was gone.

The rows of printers, at the side of the console, sprung into life and slowly plans for many machines and buildings started to appear. The Professor anxiously grabbed the first printout before looking through it and shaking his head,

"Well I will be damned. We were right all along," he said under his breath.

Marshall waited for the Professor to look at the plans and turn to him and sure enough it wasn't long before he did. With a smile to match the biggest lottery winner he started to explain the drawings to Marshall.

"You remember when I told you of the incredible 1933 Worlds Fair?" asked the professor

"Yes I do," replied Marshall.

"Well that confounded Skyride was the answer all along! It is a slightly different plan for the towers but in general we have got to build the same thing!" shrieked a very excited professor.

"How are we going to build that?" asked Marshall.

"We are going to convince America to build a modern day Worlds Fair on a bigger and grander scale than ever before. In that fair they will build the new skyride." Answered a very confident Professor.

"How are we going to do that? There is only two of us and the last time I looked we are in Swadlincote and America is a very long way away!" said Marshall effectively asking and answering his own question.

"My boy! Slow down. Firstly there is not only two of us, we have the others as well and secondly, I have spent the last ten years training you to be one of the worlds best minds. What we need to do is pool our resources and the answers will come."

The professor placed his hand on Marshall's shoulder, as he looked him straight in the eye before adding:

"The answers are always there Marshall, we just need to make people ask the questions"

"Science will accelerate at an incredible rate through the eighties and nineties. They are going to want better computer's, cars, mobile phones and this thing called the internet will be everywhere. You, Marshall are going to be at the very fore front of it all, turning out better and more desirable products everyday"

"How?" asked Marshall who was feeling like he did all those many years ago.

"You alone are going to drip feed the science community with new ideas, until they think you are a god amongst men! You will take no credit directly but you will hide behind the façade of a bigger organisation, which we will start, when it gets noticed so will you. Then the government will want some of it as well. We will pick the moment and then you will advise them on what you want built!"

"Where am I going to get the ideas from?" asked Marshall.

"You aren't going to do it alone my old friend, me and my old colleague Frank Farley are going to keep loading the gun and you will simply have to pull the trigger!"

"Sounds simple!" said Marshall rather sarcastically.

"Of course it is my boy! We will start a corporation called the Stromberg Institute, which will be based in America. Via my connections we will recruit the brightest people on the planet. This institute will be drip fed by you with new revolutionary ideas that they will think they have developed. This information will in turn be fed to the Government who will snap it up like crocodiles eating meat! You will become the link between the others and the President and ensure that we build whatever we need."

"How will I get them to build anything?" asked Marshall who felt that he was being press-ganged into service by the Professor.

The Professor laughed and pointed at the satellite dish that still sat proudly at the end of the driveway before adding,

"If I could get a British Government to build that in 1948 then you can get the Americans to build anything!"

Marshall left school in the summer of 1989 with a host of qualifications under his belt and a knowledge that he wasn't going to progress down the usual route of university and then a manager's position in some faceless company. He was going to open the biggest research company in the world and no-one was more shocked than his parents when he announced at the age of seventeen that he was not only moving to America but he had also secured over thirty million pounds of investment.

The location of the institute was to be at a location that had been drilled into Marshall from a very early age. Chicago presented an excellent centre for the development of the institute and after a short search the ideal building was found. The laboratories and research stations were set up over the first few months and Marshall began recruiting the brightest students he could find from all over the world. Within twelve months the institute was fully manned and they had been given basic ideas to research and develop into marketable products.

These ideas were in fact transcripts from the many broadcasts that had taken place over the last three hundred years. The Professor had copies of every transmission and passed the data onto Marshall on a monthly basis. Marshall would read through this data and duly pass it on to one of the many teams that now worked for him within the institute. This would in turn produce the plans for many groundbreaking ideas that could be sold to companies all around the world. Unfortunately some of the developments would end up being used for military purposes but many more would be used for peaceful purposes.

Over the first decade the institute presented many fantastic developments to the world. Everything from the Internet to modern mobile telephones and services were developed in the many rooms of the institute with the many scientists each claiming that they had developed the idea from their own imagination. Of course, controlling it all was Marshall and the Professor who continuously drip-fed their workers with increasingly complicated alien technology.

The institute rapidly became the biggest organisation of its kind on Earth and all the top technology companies would pay vast sums of money in order to be the first to use the inventions that were on offer. The last partnership that was formed was with the Government. They had watched closely as this seemingly invincible organisation had slowly fed all the top companies with world beating ideas that seemed to come from nowhere. The initial contact, as predicted by the Professor, was by the CIA and the FBI who investigated the company and Marshall for any wrong doings. The tax was paid, the paperwork was in order and all the workers were being legitimately employed. This business, at least on the surface, was just a group of scientists who were producing great ideas that could be developed into fantastic products that could in turn provide a better life for everyone.

Once they had been researched they were asked by the Government to form a relationship where the technology could be shared if it was of a relevant nature for either military or public usage. This formed that last part of the Professors plan and finally established Marshall as a named adviser to the President who would provide guidance on major technological issues. The Presidential team would contact the institute and call on Marshall whenever help or advice was needed. This could be anything from the routing of new sewer systems to the protection of America from rogue missiles. The institute provided the answers whenever they were called upon and quickly became a major part of any of the governments in power.

Marshall was quickly recognised as one of the most intelligent and forward-thinking people on the planet. He would shun all publicity and appeared to be quite happy for large companies with recognisable figureheads to take all the credit for his inventions. The Presidential teams would turn to him when required but he was careful not to become to well known with the heads of state until the time was right for him to come to the forefront. He didn't know when that would be but he knew the others would guide him when they felt the time was right.

Mr Waters Mechanical Counting Machine.

Mr Waters was an unknown inventor in the late nineteenth century. In his workshop on one hot summers day he didn't know it but he invented the most basic form of computer. Well he invented a mechanical counting machine that could differentiate between the numbers one and zero, which is the basis for binary code. What he developed would turn out to be the grandfather of all modern day computers. His mechanical calculator was large, cumbersome and quite a slow machine but it was also represented a technological masterpiece for its time. To build that machine, at that time, was no mean feat but remained a million light years away from the computers of today.

In the months running up to the time he built the machine his dreams had been disturbed. This culminated one summer night when he had the clearest most accurate dream he could ever remember. When he woke the design for the machine was engraved into his memory, he didn't have to write anything down, as he already knew it. He knew every detail of the machine and felt that he had not only seen the design but actually used it as well. It was in his head as a three-dimensional model that when he closed his eyes he could view from any angle and also dismantle. The technology was something he couldn't decipher immediately but generations of his successors would realise its importance.

He didn't know it but he was the first person in the universe to experience 'Mind-blast technology'. This was Frank Farley's magnificent development for learning and communication that he had used many times on his planet but had never connected it to the galactic link. It was originally used for young children so they would never have to attend school but would be 'plugged in' at night and then they could develop ideas within the daytime. They could also have more time for leisure. As was demanded on his planet extra leisure time resulted in happier people. Happier people meant a better and more productive planet. These facts to Frank and his department presented a win win situation, and showed the first real tangible development from his department for many years.

The ideas flowed from the children like water cascading over a waterfall. These ideas could be fed back into the machine that would then transmit the ideas to the population. This would result in millions of people using their combined brainpower to explore and develop these ideas immediately. The random, and sometimes bizarre, ideas of children presented a massive technological step forward for Franks' planet because no one had ever told a child what was and wasn't possible. The people would not invest any more time or money in the old method of dreaming up ideas. When the ability to present a complete idea within hours with the working plans was un-veiled, it moved the goal posts of development completely. The children's dreams and ideas moved the technology on the planet forward at an incredible rate of progress. Any of the children's workable ideas could be developed, tested and improved instantly. They dreamt of everything from flying cars to telekinesis and in a very short period of time anything and everything was possible.

What no one could ever imagine was what a little boy, whilst out building castles in his sandpit, thought of whilst daydreaming. He thought that if we could beam information all the way across the universe to a little blue green planet and land it on a desk, then surely we could also send an idea straight into anyone's head. Obviously, he thought, we would have to make them think it was their idea but it could be a great way of passing information and getting them to advance educationally without the need for transport.

What this little boy had developed was ' Interstellar Mind Blast' whilst playing in his sand pit one cloudy afternoon. He instantly sent Frank the plans via his thought process and then got on with much more important things, like going to play football with his waiting friends.

Frank received this information and then spent the following week adding this new 'interstellar transmitter' to the already tried and tested 'mind blast' machine. After some preliminary tests over smaller distances he tasked his team with finding a target on Earth. After a short search his researchers came up with Mr Waters. He was, in their opinion, a more than capable and willing candidate.

Mr Waters was sat quietly reading a book in his garden when he was hit by the 'mindblast'. He didn't feel anymore than a sharp pinprick on the top of his head that he put down to the many flying insects that had surrounded his chair. He didn't know what had happened until that night when he settled for a good nights sleep. It was whilst he was dreaming the whole idea downloaded into his conscious state. Frank and his team had sent him the basic plans for the super computer and the silicon chip. Mr Waters understood his bizarre dream and to the best of his knowledge he had thought of a brilliant and progressive idea.

He would never know how he thought of it, it just happened that night.

As much as the mindblast technology was a brilliant idea it was also a very dangerous weapon. If the person receiving the blast was unable to decipher the information then their brain would rapidly overload and cause a massive stroke that would normally be fatal. There was also a more sinister and dangerous side to the machine, which meant Frank, knew that it could never be given to Earth. The machine could be used to start and determine the course of conflicts. Earths dark history proved to the others of man's love of war and weapons. For this reason alone the technology was considered too dangerous, even for the others, for regular usage and was not to be used without the complete permission of the whole population of Franks' planet.

Frank was forced to lock it in a vault and forget about it for a while.

Some one hundred years later when he spoke with Marshall for the first time he instantly knew how the old machine could be used to help them to achieve their dream. The machine would help but lots of other criteria would have to be met before he would be allowed to communicate directly with Earth again.

He started communicating with Marshall as they decided on a Worlds Fair of massive proportions to bring together mankind and try to finally bring peace to Earth. This was the only way the people of Frank's planet would ever deal with Earth again. They together designed the fair and after confirming a working design finally Frank sent over details of the receiver. Instantly Marshall recognised it as the 'Skyride' from the Worlds Fair 1933. Marshall was concerned about the design and he questioned Frank about its suitability but was assured over and over again that the plans were correct and it was a fully working transmitter.

After they had finalised the plans Marshall raised the issue with Frank about the building of the Worlds Fair, and more specifically how was he supposed to build this huge project from his lowly position behind the fence in middle England.

Frank knew exactly what to do next.

On that fateful night Frank unlocked and fired up the mindblast machine. He knew he was breaking the law and he also knew how potentially dangerous it was, but he knew in his heart that he had to take a chance. Frank acquired his target and the machine beamed the basic plans, for the fair, over the galaxy and straight into the sleeping Presidents' brain. That was the night that the President had his dream to build the Worlds Fair and do his bit to try to alter mankind's future.

It was also the night Marshall woke at three in the morning and packed his bags, left the institute, and boarded a flight to Washington. In doing so he waved goodbye to his old life. He attended the White House a week later and, exactly to Franks plan, there was a position waiting for him at that fateful meeting as one of the scientific advisors. It was a day later that Marshall first spoke with the President at the meeting that started the ball rolling on the construction of the fair, a fair that was set to stun the modern world.

Marshall received a mind blast as well that day but he would have never known, as it was just a subtle push to make him do something. The Professor had been telling him what was required for years so all Frank did was effectively move the plan along a bit quicker. It was Frank who urged Marshall forward in that meeting when he first spoke to the President.

Frank dutifully took the mind blast machine and carefully locked it away. He knew he was the only person on his planet to ever break the law and he also knew that he would never be forgiven for interfering in Earths history again. All contact with Earth had been disallowed forever after the development and use of the first nuclear weapon on Hiroshima.

Frank was taking a tremendous personal risk. He just hoped against all hope that the people of Earth would repay his faith in them.

As for Mr Waters and his incredible counting machine, they did not fair so well against the cynical scientific community. After demonstrating its incredible speed and accuracy at adding and dividing numbers he was thrown out of his college position for being no more than a magical circus act. His reputation in tatters he sold his workshop and machine to a former colleague and spent the rest of his days working in a brickyard.

He would often have vivid and disturbing dreams regarding his machine and would spend many waking hours doodling designs on old bits of paper. As he neared retirement he was stunned to read of a famous scientist who had invented a basic computer. He watched in disbelief as this scientist received critical acclaim for showing the world his mechanical counting machine.

Sometimes the credit for genius is credited to the best salesperson instead of the inventor.

Chapter 10

Return to behind the fence.

Marshall knew he had to return behind the fence to complete the plans for the Worlds Fair and he knew this would raise questions but he couldn't reveal the fence yet. All this would achieve is to add to the confusion and the last thing he and the presidents needed was more questions or public outcry.

The pub still held many great memories for Marshall although it had changed hands many times over the years it was still there. Marshall always looked at it as he did when he was child, indeed now when he returned it reminded him of his mum and dad and the fantastic summer nights he would spend there playing. Of course it would also remind him of that fateful night when he looked through that little gap. A little gap, which he had subsequently found out, that, was actually engineered into the fence to allow the right person to look through. All they needed was an open mind and he was the one who possessed it.

He walked past the pub and into the back garden, it was still as he remembered it, perfectly oval and the fence was still there looking exactly as it did all those years ago. Marshall climbed up onto the cinder path and walked round until he reached panel five. He turned around and looking sideways he saw the gap and with no effort whatsoever wandered through.

Marshall moved down the embankment and walked slowly towards the laboratory down the moss-covered roadway that had lost its man-made look. The displays had aged more now as the many years of being open to the changing British weather had taken its toll on the unfinished buildings. Some of the displays had fallen down as they had lost their battle against the elements and let gravity take its course; others had survived by letting the plants help them to support their weight. Marshall walked towards the dish and turned to climb the creaking steps of the laboratory as he opened the old door he noted the smell and remembered again that first day he had ventured behind the fence.

Inside only one thing had changed, the professor was no longer there. He had become progressively ill in the nineties and passed away just two days after the start of the new millennium. He always promised Marshall that he would see the new year of what he believed would be the start of mans greatest millennium and as always he wasn't wrong. He was one hundred and two years old and as bright and articulate as he had his final conversation as the day Marshall first met him. Marshall missed him he was a mentor and more over a friend, he hoped that wherever he was now that he would be looking down and smiling as Marshall slowly built his dream.

The banks of computers and transmitters in the old laboratory now looked even more antiquated as they represented a bygone era in size and processing power. Indeed the smart phone that Marshall had in his pocket probably had more computing power than most of the machines in the room, but it lacked one important detail. The man who built this transmitter was a genius and no amount of companies, shareholders and production lines can ever match that.

Genius just happens naturally and along with years of experience cannot be bought at any cost. Often Marshall would wonder what the Professor could have achieved with the technology that was now available, perhaps he could have built a link to the others on his own, but one thing was for certain he wouldn't have spent all his time making ringtones like so many of today's self titled geniuses. The Professor was still dreaming of more extravagant ideas when he died, so many of today's inventors only think of their bank account once they have had a good idea.

Marshall walked over to the power switches on the right hand side of the room, which from the window overlooked the transmitter. Like so many times before, since the Professors death, he held the master power switch and slowly pressed down until it gave out a large clunk and fired power to the many old machines. As always when he did this he closed his eyes and always prayed that they would work, as, even after all these years, he hadn't a clue how to fix them if they went wrong.

The machines immediately sprung into life with a loud whirr of fans and buzzes of age-old processors being driven by valves, not microchips that he had gotten use to. The printers behind him immediately started churning out many directions and instructions for the building of the Worlds Fair. Marshall felt it was as if the machines had been waiting for him to switch them on and were in some way glad to see him again. The plans for this fair were exhaustive, not only had the others planned the halls and displays within they had also planned for water supplies, sewage and transport links to the site.

The plans showed the skyride and underneath it stretching out over the area was a technological feast showing everything from robotic surgery to new and exciting transport ideas. All of which was new and all of which Marshall had to convince the President was achievable. He knew he couldn't do this alone and planned to gradually drip-feed these fantastic new ideas into the institute over the next few years. The plans were very precise and presented for the first time a timetable and workable diagram of what to do next.

As Marshall sat looking at the plans his concentration was broken by the incessant noise of the communication alarm. This was basically a flashing light and buzzer, which alerted anyone present to the fact that our galactic friends had sent a voice message for them to listen to and act upon. Marshall had no idea how it worked what went on or how they knew someone was available but it always seemed to happen when he sat down to relax for a while. He reached forward and pressed the communication button and immediately the machine sprung into life like it was eager to reveal the recording.

What proceeded was a recorded message, which Frank had sent only one minute previously:

'Hello Marshall. Good to see work is progressing well. Please build exactly as the plans and we will see you then. Also make this a show worth attending! Get as many of the human race to watch that night and we guarantee they will also open their minds like you did all those years ago. Get the machines built and ready for July 2020. Time of day is irrelevant as once the link is established we will be joined forever. I look forward to visiting earth but before we arrive I will be making sure they don't shoot me! Regards Frank Farley II.' Marshall gulped and really wished he was not involved in the whole thing, it had grown with him since he was a child and now the reality of it all was hitting him like a runaway express train. He alone was going to be responsible for linking two races together and also revealing this fact to the world.

After spending a week behind the fence Marshall had analysed the plans and prepared his presentation. He was as ready as he would ever be and knew it was time to fly back to America and leave the comfort of his known life. Once the fair commenced and the link had been established he knew his life would never be the same again. He also knew that the area behind the fence would have finally fulfilled its purpose and would become obsolete. With a degree of sadness he collected his things together and for one last time downloaded all the data from the systems onto his laptop computer. He looked around the room as he reached out for the power switch and as he closed the switch he involuntarily spoke out to his old friend;

"Goodbye Professor, you served mankind well. I will do you proud".

With this he turned and walked out the laboratory and closed the door for the last time. He walked through the rows of mostly derelict displays, which would never be finished and climbed the cinder bank all the way to the fence. He turned and looked over the whole site. The banner was still intact, if not a little rustier, and could still be read. He remembered the first time he stood in this very spot and couldn't help but shed a tear for absent friends who would not see the culmination of his life's work. As he looked down he could still make out the footprints of the young boy who stood here on a warm sunny afternoon many years ago. He turned and saw on the fence the remains of motorcycle flag, which he had put there many years previously, to remind him where the gap was. He reached for it and before putting it safely in his case he carefully folded it. Without looking back he climbed through the gap and back into the pub garden, for the very last time before everything would change.

A meeting was scheduled between all the necessary parties to decide upon a location for the fair. Marshall knew he would have to convince the President and his advisers of the benefits of basing the fair in Chicago. He prepared a written statement that showed the benefits of the transport systems and the open park that historically had presented the 1933 Worlds Fair to international applause. Marshall had also prepared working diagrams and models of events that could be seen to have a great relevance to modern society as well as trying to regenerate the excitement of the original fair. The plans involved many halls which would allow countries of the world space to show the paying public their dreams and technologies. Centre to the whole fair would be an exact copy of the 1933 Skyride. This towering transporter bridge would allow people to not only move from the main land to the island but also afford magnificent views of the fair and downtown Chicago. They would be moved along the cable on fantastic futuristic space cars. These would not only present a luxurious and retro journey across the sky but also look and feel like the predicted space ships of old. The type that appeared in the early space films which were all fins and sparkling flashing lights. These would glide along the ropes accompanied by a soundtrack of roaring engines and fake exhaust smoke, billowing from the rocket engines at the back of the hull.

The only thing about the space craft type cars that the public didn't know was that they were a lot closer to space ships than they could have been imagined. They were a distinct and specific design, by the others, which would enable a transitional journey between the planets. The cable car design would make a suitable landing strip allowing for the cars to slow and be dismounted safely above the earth. As always the biggest danger on transportation was fire, which had proved time and again to be the nemesis of providing the link between the planets.

This they had found out all those years ago at the Crystal Palace when the result of re-entry into this dimension from the trans-galactic loop was massive amounts of heat and fire. These newly designed cars would allow the occupants to arrive safely cocooned inside the fireproofed and cooled interiors. The distance from the ground would allow the air to cool them without the risk of fire spreading. The biggest problem with this was the apparent failure of this to work, but no one could deny the fact that something had happened, on that cold night, as the cars had disappeared and new ones from our galactic friends had arrived.

The design that Marshall had was nearly an exact copy of the original skyride, in fact the design was so incredibly close that Marshall even questioned what on earth he had been sent and even if this had been some kind of mistake, but he had been assured this was correct and not only that but it was perfect. It would work. It would allow transport of individuals, data and technology between the two planets and it was tried, tested and a working model. How the others knew this was beyond Marshalls understanding but their confidence was unerring.

All Marshall had to do was convince the President to build it, and judging by the amount of interest by private businessmen and government officials from many departments, he would be able to convince them to build anything. They eagerly looked at his plans for the fair and were very impressed by not only the detail of the buildings and attractions but also the incredible detail that had been placed on making the fair economical and environmentally friendly.

All he had to do now was get the go ahead for his location and the rest would make history.

Chapter 11.

The Build.

Marshall and the President were rapidly forming a formidable team. Marshalls incredible grasp of science and planning and the Presidents undeterred enthusiasm for his Worlds Fair, not to mention his access to Americas' incredibly deep pockets, had seen them form a friendship that was as efficient as it was open. Each sharing a mutual respect for the others needs and a determination to make this the best worlds fair that has ever been seen.

Ensuring the fair was built correctly and efficiently was key to the success of not only the fair but also for Marshall's own plans. The sites, for the fair, were suggested by a public opinion poll and Marshall would have to sell his own personal choice of Chicago to the public through a series of live television debates. Although this was second nature to the President and the other candidates, Marshall had found his newfound fame a little overpowering. Marshall had spent most of his adult life behind the fence with only the Professor for company, and so to suddenly be thrust in front of millions of television viewers was a huge challenge. Luckily he could draw on the vast experience of those around him to present a good case for his preferred site.

An early front-runner in the polls was Washington, as everyone in the government thought that the Worlds biggest show of all time should be in the capital. Marshall had the enviable task of convincing the President to hold the Fair at the original site of the 1933 Worlds Fair, not least of all because the 'Skyride' had to be built in exactly the same place as the original. This would enable a direct link with the others, as it had been the only site in history that had been even marginally successful.

The televised meeting to decide the placement of the fair came around all to soon. Marshall never ceased to be amazed by the Government. To the general public this was an open telephone vote where they all decided the location of the fair. In reality the decision was made behind closed doors nearly a month before the public telephone vote had even started. Of course the viewers would have to register their votes via a premium rate phone line, which would generate money for the government to spend. This money, he found out later, helped to finance the construction of the fair and also pay some of the advisers their huge costs.

"This public vote will decide the location of Mankind's biggest and most impressive Worlds Fair!" the President stated to the cameras as he opened the meeting with a furor. The television companies had jumped at this chance to air this public vote. This was mainly down to the massive advertising revenue that could be gained by having any live debate where the President was involved.

"We must decide what is the most accessible, usable and most importantly profitable place to build the fair and also we must discuss how we are going to attract people from all over the World," he continued. The public vote took place over the next twelve hours with interludes of music and advertising. The revenue was huge and at the end of the evening the President announced to the waiting public that Chicago had been voted for by the public.

The meeting to decide this had taken place a month earlier and had involved Marshall gaining the support he needed to push forward the location he required.

Dr Wang was the current overseas minister and a very powerful figure within Congress. All the parties involved knew that he would carry a huge amount of votes and were listening intently for his decision as to where he would personally prefer to see the fair. This was very convenient for Marshall as he was an old friend from university, but they hadn't had a meaningful conversation for many years.

"Hello Wang"; started a rather sheepish Marshall as he approached the Doctor.

"Ah, young Marshall. Where have you been hiding yourself away since university?" replied Wang.

"Oh you know", replied Marshall, "This and that!" he added with a smile.

"I have heard that you have been very busy indeed!" chortled a smiling Wang as he pointed towards the President, who was sat in front of a large plan of the Skyride.

"Well you know me Wang! I never could resist a challenge!" laughed a concerned Marshall. He was only concerned because his old friend seemed to be more than a little interested in the Skyride.

"I hope you don't mind me saying, but in these days of virtual reality and the like, it just seems like a very old fashioned thing to build at a fair which is supposed to represent the progress of mankind", answered Wang as he gestured towards the picture, "these types of rides were a great thing back in the old days but now every child can ride the skies on their computer or games console, indeed, three dimensional television makes you feel like your there! so a big cable car type contraption is a very bizarre way of attracting visitors"

Marshall thought for a moment and then answered. "To play a game is one thing. But the thrill of flying through the sky whilst looking down on the people cannot be replicated by any computer. Children and adults alike will marvel at the noise and views as they apparently fly through the air over the river and land on the island, which will house all the pavilions of the future. It will feel like they have not only had a ride in the sky but have also flown into the future".

All the time Marshall was saying this he kept thinking about everyone's reaction as they finally realized what the ride was actually for. He hoped that they would understand why he had to keep it secret but he also hoped that the President would forgive him for his many half-truths.

Wang looked at Marshall and reached out a hand. Marshall accepted the handshake with some trepidation and looked Wang straight in the eye.

Wang took what seemed like an eternity to reply before saying "Marshall, we have a lot of history. I remember fondly sitting with you at school in our Physics class whilst you questioned everything that was being said by our flustered teacher. I also remember the shock on our tutors face when you found some old theories wrong at the tender age of twelve! The laughs we had in the common room have never left me and the feeling that I was friends with someone who one day was going to make a difference."

Wang waved to bring the President nearer as he finished.

"You could do a lot worse than do whatever Marshall says, he is a gifted and talented individual. He will not get this wrong... Chicago should be the home of the 2020

Worlds Fair. I will personally recommend this to congress."

Marshall smiled and thanked his old friend for his recommendation and continued loyalty.

This original meeting converged and it was soon recognised that it would be over very quickly. The President stood up and after only a short introduction turned and addressed the heads of all the services required to build the fair.

"We have made a quick and meaningful decision for the location of the Worlds Fair…

We will hold the Biggest Worlds Fair in history at the preferred site of Chicago!" he finished with a flourish.

There were no questions from the attendees just a muted round of applause and then the planning needed to begin a this fair needed to built in only a short period of time.

Marshall was placed in overall control of the Fair. He answered only to the President, with whom he would have weekly meetings with. All the armed forces would work hand in hand with a plethora of private contractors in the rapid construction of the site. Many of these private contractors worked for companies mainly owned by people in congress and Marshall could see that he was going to be responsible for making some people very rich. The designs for the pavilions would be tendered to individual countries and the land allocated on a price per acre basis, the more extravagant the pavilion the more these countries would have to pay. The whole team was very aware that even though this was for the people it would still have to make enough money to pay for itself and hopefully provide a healthy profit as well. The attendees would need to be catered for and all the food franchises would be sold off to the highest bidders and everything, right down to litterbins, would be available for sponsorship. Everything that was except for the 'skyride' this would be paid for by the government and would be free for the people to use. The towering ride would transport hundreds of people at a time over to the island of the future.

Over the next two years the area around Peace Park in Chicago would once again be the home to the greatest show on the planet. The development would be built with sympathy to the environment and utilize, where it could, the surrounding natural environment. Wind, solar and wave power would provide the energy required and the rainwater would be caught and used.

This was mankind's chance to show off the best technology available and the governments of the world were quickly grasping the chance with both hands. The developments sprung up quickly and efficiently.

Most of all Marshall watched in awe as the armed forces, so often used by men in power to cause destruction, built the magnificent skyride. The shining towers slowly rose out of the earth to dominate the skyline of this part of Chicago. In 1933 they were the tallest structures in the city, however, in these modern times they were dwarfed by some of the skyscrapers. They did provide a fantastic view over the area and would give the fair goers a handsome viewpoint to take in the greatness of this mighty fair.

All too soon the cars were being lifted into position and the fair was rapidly nearing completion. The final touches for the skyride were two huge antennae, which topped each tower and were the only discernable difference between the new and old rides.

They were very thinly disguised to the general public as mobile telephone masts.

But only Marshall knew different.

In total contrast to Marshall the President was having a torrid time trying to explain to the Worlds governments and media what was going on and why? He wanted to tell them about his incredible dream and how clear it was but he would have been labeled a crank and driven from office. Instead he called a worldwide media conference where he would discuss the fair and also explain the removal of foreign military assistance.

Only a short time after announcing Chicago as the holder of the Worlds Fair he was being challenged in court regarding the telephone voting, which had quickly turned into a scandal. The reason for this scandal was one of the opposition had found a leaked document which clearly showed that New York had won the publics backing. It also stated that the decision for Chicago was taken a month previously. The Presidents advisers were looking into the leak and he had been assured that there would be answers soon.

On the day of the press conference the President was informed that the head of the telesales company, a certain Mr. Thomas Smythe, had firstly put on record that the leaked document was a fake and he released details of the correct voting, which clearly showed the city of Chicago as a winner. Secondly, he had resigned as CEO of Pop-top Telesales and committed his entire salary and bonus to the Worlds Fair building fund. The President knew this was all false. He also knew that history told him that this, probably innocent man and his family, were in grave danger of not surviving long enough to change his mind over the statement. This injustice was a price he was prepared to pay to keep his office and the poor mans situation didn't even enter his conscience.

The conference was packed with reporters from all over the World as well as representatives from the United Nations. The President walked on stage and took a deep breath. This gave him time to clear his mind and remember why he took this job in the first place.

"Good Morning people of the world." Great start he thought to himself before continuing, "Thank you for gathering here today and listening to myself explaining the actions of the United States".
There was a deathly quiet in the room as the sharp dizziness of stage fright stirred in the Presidents stomach.

"We decided one year ago to remove all military assistance and foreign policing from all countries, which for decades we have supported and assisted in peacekeeping.

The reasons for this are simple. We, as a Country, could no longer justify the expense and risks to our men and women. All the people of the world need to stand up and take responsibility for their own borders and security. Not one country is further at risk because of our withdrawal than our own and we will defend ourselves if required.

We will defend our borders with vigor. If any countries or organizations see this as a show of weakness or an act of cowardice then they will be greatly surprised by our response.

The money from these services will be diverted to build the greatest worlds fair of all time. This will promote and advertise world trade also it will showcase the fantastic developments, which at present adorn the shelves of laboratories, to the public. Indeed it is time to move mankind forward without the shackles of war and hatred.

Our forefathers dreamt of a world filled with technology and easier living. We will rebuild this dream and develop technology, which works and is available to everyone. The best computers will no longer be the premise of the rich and famous. Every citizen will have access to the most advanced technologies available. We will explore the alternative energy markets and develop a worthy successor to fossil fuels.

In brief, Ladies and Gentlemen, we are going to lead the way to a better life for all of mankind. Not only for today but also for every tomorrow in every country of the World.

It starts right here. Chicago Worlds Fair 2020 will display the best of every country on the planet. Every country will be able to showcase itself and be part of our new dream"

With this a large detailed plan of the Worlds Fair and a presentation on multiple screens began to show what the fair was all about.

"I am not taking questions", continued the President

"The decision has already been made and we as a country are going to once again lead the World"

With this the President turned and left the stage to applause from the crowd. There was talking amongst the guests and the general feeling was positive but some, as always, couldn't understand how or why this had happened. It was totally out of character for a country that had heavily been involved in policing so many nations had suddenly stopped and totally changed direction. The implications could be many but the flipside of this all would be a billion dollars a month being spent on research and not war. The possibilities of this research and development could be endless and the slideshow on the plasma screens showed how the money was going to be redistributed. The space programme would receive a full budget for the first time in decades with the lunar programme and the Mars projects being reopened. All American laboratories and hospitals were to be allocated huge amounts into research to combat and defeat serious illnesses. Most importantly to Marshall was the Worlds Fair would receive all the labor and cash it needed to develop into not only a show in Chicago but also an event that could be held more often. In-between fairs there would be shows, which would be moved around America, along with a permanent travelling display of modern 'Dream-liners'. These could be used to tour the globe, bringing technology and developments to everyone who wanted to see them.

While these announcements were taking place just a few miles away Mr Smyth and his family were enjoying a quiet break on the family boat, whilst they tried to plan how to rebuild their lives after the public humiliation of an innocent man. Ironically during the Presidents speech about the scandal their boat suddenly and without warning listed and sank quickly into the cold Atlantic Ocean. Everyone on board drowned that day taking with them any risk of the truth ever being revealed.

As much as things were changing, some things stayed the same.

Liberty

The American President stood in utter disbelief as he listened to yet another bizarre request that he had just received from the British Prime Minister who had just walked into his office after enduring a torturous Atlantic crossing.

"Would you like to repeat what you have just said?" requested the President.

"Certainly old chap!" replied the Prime Minister before continuing "We, and the others, require you to build a four hundred feet tall copper and asbestos tower on the shores of the area you call New York. It's a dastardly plan to help them to be able to land here and finally achieve our long tried aim for a inter-planetary link"

The President stood motionless and quietly tried to gather his confused thoughts.

"I don't know what you lot are on, but over here we are not exactly flush with money to keep building these follies. After all anything good that ever comes out of it you lot keep for yourselves and your blasted Empire! If you don't start sharing then we are not building anymore!" said the President who knew he would have to take a firm stance on these matters or risk building yet another pointless monument.

"Oh there is no denying the fact that the Empire has benefitted from the fantastic alien technology. We have many horseless carriages; steamboats and our cotton mills are the envy of the world! But we are led to believe that they have to build here in America because you are far better aligned to their star. So I agree, with a heavy heart, that I accept that some sharing will have to take place between your young upstart of a country and our mighty empire," replied the patriotic Prime Minister.

The President looked his old friend in the eye, and whilst ignoring his demeaning comment, a wry smile started to crack across his aged face as he realised that Great Britain would no longer have the monopoly over the fantastic ideas that followed the inevitable failure of these missions.

"I only have one small problem," continued the President whilst he was surveying the complicated plans that were laid out before him, "The public are not going to buy into an idea where a great big copper aerial is erected over probably one of the greatest man-made skylines ever!"

The Prime Minister took on board what his compatriot was saying and thought for a moment before adding:

"Well you could do what we have always done and dress it up as a statue and pretend, to the public, that someone else paid for it!"

"What the public doesn't know won't hurt them." He added with a wink.

The Prime Minister closed the meeting and after a few more pleasantries he returned to his ocean liner and set sail that very night, after probably the shortest state visit in history. The paying customers on that boat never even knew the Prime Minister was on board as the whole journey was veiled in the usual secrecy.

The President went back to his many advisers and the very next day the public were informed that the country was to be 'given' a statue, from France, to help them to celebrate their independence. This would be built on the harbour in New York and would be a marvellous sight for the people on all the many liners that would be approaching America, for the first time, via this busy route.

Five years later the 'Statue of Liberty' was unveiled in New York harbour to the amazement of the people of the world. The French government who pretended it was a gift in return for some old warships and the British government who showed great support for the Independence celebrations supported this. As originally predicted by the President on the day of transmission nothing happened and not long afterwards the paperwork and written apology duly arrived on the Prime Ministers desk. This paperwork was immediately sent to the President who, upon its arrival, had his top scientists and advisers to look at it.

Contained in the paperwork were plans for a better design of motorcar, which was forwarded to a young entrepreneur who the President only knew as Henry. Plans for efficient hydroelectric power generators that were passed to the highest bidding power company and a strange system for sharing information that the others called the 'internet'. The scientists took this idea away and spent many years working on the strange, unearthly design.

Later the same day the President stood in his bedroom and, after pouring himself a strong drink, he commenced in unfolding the apology and read it in some wonder. It simply read:

'You built the wrong thing! We asked for an aerial not a statue please try and build to the plans next time as otherwise it wont work. As a symbol of our continued support for the people of Earth please accept these basic plans for improving your lives. Regards Frank.

P.s. Use some caution when you release the Internet to everyone as it quickly gets out of control.'

The President casually screwed up the paper and threw it into the waste paper basket in front of him.

"Just keep sending the profitable ideas you stupid Aliens!" he mumbled to himself before drinking the last of his brandy and retiring to bed.

Chapter 12.

Changing the skyline forever.

The sun slowly rose over the Chicago skyline and the beams of orange sunlight filtered down onto the fair, lighting the exhibits and giving the area a homely warm glow that slowly lit the windows of Marshall's office. He had set up his office at the westerly end of the fair construction site, this gave him a panoramic view of the buildings as they seemingly rose out of the old park land like tulips breaking through the soil in early spring.

Marshalls office was laid out like his old laboratory with papers and computers strewn everywhere and whiteboards full of notes and ramblings. His desk was adorned with two pictures, one of the professor and the other of his parents. All three of them looked back at him with the smiles he remembered so well. His computer would regularly do a very good job of reminding him that he was in charge as his e-mail alert would sound and the screen would present him with more questions and comments from the various members of the presidential team. He kept a close eye on all the buildings but in particular he would have daily updates from the construction team who were building the skyride. He knew that any mistakes or cut corners at this stage could reduce his attempt to the growing rank of also ran's that had littered the last three hundred years.

When his duties would let him he would leave his office and wander around the site and take in some of the many marvels that were already on display within the various buildings. The countries of the world had taken a keen interest in the trade benefits of such an exhibition and due to the already massive amount of interest that was already been shown by the public, this was already being billed as 'The show to end all shows'. The advertising benefits were plain to see, there were going to be millions of visitors over the course of the show and once they had entered the fair it was effectively a closed market. Where money was to be made then the major companies would not be far away, and their investment was crucial in making this fair a success. The publics' imagination had been lit up by the promises that this fair held and a frenzy of excitement was building at the presence of something special that everyone was invited to attend. For the first time in history the area surrounding Chicago was enjoying one hundred per cent employment and the eyes of the World, via news channels, visited daily. The financial markets had seen a slight turnaround already as the public finally began to believe that they had something to aim towards again. On a global scale the inventions that were on show, and the potential financial gains, in Chicago were already generating huge interest and the show was not even open yet. This all boded well for the overall show and also for the incredible announcement that would stun the world when it finally happened.

The technology already revealed had far outreached the current assumed levels of development, so much so that questions were being asked were at the top levels of various governments and monarchies around the world as to whether contact with the others had been made again. This was mainly an informed guess by those who still knew of the original dialogues between the planets. The rules that had been installed before 1950 had stated that all nations would have a requirement to inform the United Nations of any contact with the others. This was taken so seriously that a web-based camera had been installed at Downing Street viewing the exact location that the 'paperwork' would normally arrive. Of course, what everyone didn't know was that there was one person on the planet that was in regular contact and he was involved at the highest levels of government.

Although the survivors of those days were few it was enough for some countries to dispatch spies to try and ascertain whether the Americans had indeed had 'contact'. The reports from these spies were mainly restricted to who had really thought of the ideas and where they had come from, however, one spy had followed the lead scientist back to a small pub in England. The spy had followed Marshall all the way to the pub but by the time the spy had got to the garden Marshall had gone behind the fence. The spy had mistakenly thought he was in the pub and left without further investigation, merely able to report back to the Dutch government that nothing was untoward. Questions were also being asked all over the globe since the ceasing of all military action, but no one could deny the outbreak of peace for the first time in mans history was a welcome break, there had been many threats to break this delicate state of affairs but after two years the addiction to peace by the population of the Earth had become infectious. This Worlds Fair had become everyone's sole diversion and anyone that Marshall spoke to wanted to attend it or be part of it.

No dictator or extremist organisation could change the fact that mankind wanted peace and to progress. They had waited long enough for the promised future and this fair was the signal to the public that the people in power were listening and this was finally happening. Due to the fact that the top levels of Government appeared to be improving the country instead of wasting money the general attitude of the public had shifted. The attendance of voluntary work had increased and companies had started to invest in their workers. The general feeling was that after a long wait the future was finally here. The Promised Land of extra leisure time and less work was on the horizon and the public wanted it more than ever.

Marshall would often ascend the towers on the skyride and stand at the very top of the viewing platforms. This would give him a birds-eye view of the fair and allow him to take in its enormity. This was his work, built to an alien design that only he knew of, but it was his work that had convinced the President to invest millions of dollars and immense amounts of labour. He watched as the guide ropes were slowly lowered into position between the two towers. The cars, which would parade between the two towers, were being built by the American Space Agency to an exact specification and would be the last part of the fair to be put into place. The towers had been built by the Army, with huge investment from private business, and represented the latest standards of accuracy and strength. The buildings had used many new technologies in their construction, technology that had been directly supplied by The Stromberg Institute to the various construction companies. The only disclaimer added was that no military usage of the new materials would ever be allowed. Marshall knew that the various agencies were looking on and would have loved to have their war inducing hands on these strong, light materials. The various buildings around the site represented huge leaps in construction and sustainability. The press were doing a very good job of convincing the world that all these leaps in technology were their ideas and Marshall was happy with that. It made him realise how quickly all the inventions of old had quickly become part of society and man had never thought twice about where they had come from. Everything from the telephone to the supercomputer had been developed in incredibly small time frames that if anyone had been bothered to notice made no sense at all. Mankind had been using alien technology for hundreds of years and with the completion of this fair they would finally know it. Marshall smiled to himself and imagined the look on everyone's face as they finally found out what had been happening and he slowly slipped on his sunglasses as the bright morning sun rose high over the fair.

Often the President and members of his team would visit the site and take a tour of all the areas under construction. He would congratulate Marshall on a well ordered and organised site before making comments on things he wished to add. Marshall would take these suggestions and more often than not forget all about them but occasionally he would build something extra so the President would feel like he was in charge. The President would always feel like Marshall was one step ahead of him and on many occasions wouldn't state any desire to change a thing, only for Marshall to tell him something that he was already thinking. This would result in him being slightly confused but satisfied that Marshall was indeed the man to drive this wonderful development forward and help him to win total public support.

Exactly the same as Marshall would do, the President would also stand at the top of the towers and look down on the fair, but he wouldn't be thinking of the potential for galactic exploration, instead he would be thinking of his position of power and how he had thought of the fair in the first place. He could remember his dream that night like it was carved in stone. He only wished he could use that type of thinking to help him with other pressing issues in his political life. The economy had started to revive itself under the umbrella of positive thinking that the fair had already bought but it was only a scratch on the trillions of dollars of debt that his forerunners had so graciously left him. The position of President was one of much stress and worry but the economy was the thought that would keep him awake at night. Although this construction had not been without worry he kept having the over riding emotion that everything would be alright and the economy would be put into perspective by the imminent arrival of the greatest Worlds Fair that mankind had ever attempted to put on. All he could hope was that this brilliant and huge development would cultivate enough belief to kick start the economy as a whole and develop world trade to the point where his beloved country would recover enough to support itself again like it did in the earlier years of its development. He had heard nothing but positives from the opinion polls and his advisers had repeatedly told him of his great and noble decision to build the fair.

This was the most important development of modern times and everyone involved carried a lot of responsibility in ensuring the success and relevance of everything involved. The displays were going to present massive and permanent changes to the public and the businesses of the World. The President looked over towards the Chicago skyline and then cast his eye towards the island, which was now connected by the cables of the Skyride, and realised that he alone was altering the course of history.

How much history was going to change was something that even the President couldn't have ever estimated.

The French

The British have historically never liked or trusted the French, but then saying that the French have never really liked the British much either. When the others sent a message instructing the building of a huge receiver in the middle of Paris the British Prime Minister was naturally apprehensive. How on earth was he supposed to sell this idea to the untrusting French President? The two countries were barely on talking terms and trade had been very slow between the two nations for a number of years.

When he eventually plucked up the courage and made the call the conversation was brief and directly to the point:

"We have had a plan delivered" started an anxious Prime Minister

"Proceed," said the lofty President, who had little time for the Prime Minister or his island country.

"We need to build a huge receiver in the middle of Paris so the others can transmit to us." the Prime Minister proceeded to explain the need to build a massive tower, to an alien design, in the area of Paris.

"Ok we shall build it! Send me the plans and I will ensure that it is built exactly so." The President was airy and confident when he added, " but we want the same deal as the Americans with any plans they send for new technology"

" I take it you are presuming they fail?" asked a now angrier Prime Minister, who wanted more than anything a link to be established once and for all as this would present more benefits than a one off idea.

"Not at all but you never know what will happen!" laughed the President before adding, " They have never been reliable have they? So we want the insurance that we get the benefits of all the expense that we go to".

"Very well the plans are yours but if they succeed then we demand part of the credit after all they are our contacts!" finished the Prime Minister before he slammed the telephone down in a pointless unseen show of defiance.

The French dutifully completed the Eiffel Tower in time for the 1889 Worlds Fair. It was a raging success and everyone from the joining nations was impressed by not only its size, but also its faultless build quality and futuristic design. It seemed incredible at the time that such a feat could be completed and would stand as a testament to mans ability to build vast complex structures.

On the third day of December that very year the others informed London that the transmission would take place at eleven hundred hours. When the time came absolutely nothing happened. There was a rumour that the tip of the tower momentarily glowed blue but this stayed as a tale and no scientific proof ever emerged.

Within two days, as always, the paperwork explaining the failure arrived from the others. The French President made sure he was personally present at Downing Street to see it arrive. The relations between the two countries were so poor that he did not believe that the paperwork would be passed to him without being tampered with in some way. The static electricity in the room audibly increased and he grabbed the paperwork as soon as it landed on the desk. All that was legible on the sheets of paper was a load of equations and numbers that made no sense to him at all. In his fit of temper at the massive costs and apparent worthless reward he angrily screwed up the paper and threw it on the fire.

What he and no one else would ever know is that in his fit of temper he destroyed the plans for an anti-gravity machine that would null the use of fossil fuels for moving loads over the surface of the planet forever. The French would have led the world into a new era of transport technology.

It would have been one of the greatest discoveries of all time but it was burnt without even being looked at.

Professor Frank Farley, who was looking on from his planet, shook his head in disbelief at mans constant inability to not only make use of great technology but read and develop basic plans.

The tower was built wrong. It had not been built to the plans that had been sent. It should have had a flat landing pad at the top and a spiralling single-track road around the sides, which specially designed cars could have driven up for the show but would also have operated as a transitional antennae when used as a receiver. It was built without the road and the landing pad so would never be any use except as an ornament.

When the Prime Minister heard what had happened he just smiled to himself and carried on his daily political business. He often thought that the French President had ordered it to be built wrong on purpose so that he would receive plans for new ideas then claim that their scientists had thought of them. His greed and desire for fame had resulted in a huge failure.

The tower lived on and graced the skyline of Paris for many years after the fair and in this time more than recouped the original building costs. The real long-term cost, to the French, was not financial but the fact that they would never again be trusted to build a receiver.

Chapter 13

The opening of the Worlds Fair.

The grand opening of the Worlds Fair was an incredible event. The tickets for the first two years had sold out within two days; demand was such that tickets for the opening day were changing hands for many thousands of pounds and the businesses that were involved announced an immediate and sustained increase in sales.

Marshall stood and surveyed the waiting crowds from the gatehouse restaurant, which afforded views to the waiting areas and also over the whole fair. He couldn't help but smile when he looked over to the fantastic sky ride. Its cables and steel towers were glistening in the morning sunlight and the cars were already making their steady journey between the towers. Smoke was evacuating from the cars exhausts in a mock rocket engine effect that just added to the image of spaceships that were flying between the island and the mainland. Marshall was proud of his achievement and he hoped that the professor was looking down on his idea with pride.

The gates to the Worlds Fair 2020 opened at exactly 2020hrs on the 20th February 2020. This was the moment that the star 'Arcturus' shone down on the main building and provided a perfect line between earth and the star. As the star lined up the whole of the fair lit up and fireworks erupted over the night sky. A display of military planes of the ages flew over Chicago and the first spacecraft to be launched from the area took off, lighting the night sky with its brilliant orange flame. A flotilla of boats over the surrounding harbour sounded their horns and the waters of the harbour were lit up bright red by millions of underwater lights. The Sky ride was lit up with many thousands of lights and the cars were traced over the night sky by searchlights. The effect of it all was amazing; the crowds cheered and whooped in delight at what had been achieved.

The many displays by various nations opened with a furore and fan fare never seen before in our time. The technology and displays were incredible. The world's press were in attendance and television crews broadcast the opening all over the globe. This was special and everyone knew it. Man had achieved something special, and Marshall was right at the centre of it.

The fair progressed unabated for the first week and every day seemed to show the world a new technology that would be met with disbelief. Some of the businesses of all nations took the opportunity to display their latest and greatest products and many kept an eye in the past, reliving great moments in their history. A great addition to the fair was the return of the 'Future Liners' these were vehicles used in the forties and fifties to promote new technology to the population of America long before the advent of television. They initially toured the fair but after those first few weeks they took to the roads and promoted their wares to the entire country. On the back of their success other countries also built similar machines over the first year and put them to use showing their people the technology of tomorrow. The hope would be an increase in morale globally similar to that in Chicago. It would have seemed that the population preferred to be shown the products. Watching the developments on television was never the same as having the products in your own hands were you could use the technology as it was intended.

The global shift in attitudes was palpable. The fair had shown everyone what we were always capable of and now people wanted to know what the whole of mankind could achieve now that war and conflict appeared to be a thing of the past. The fair provided this to America and had given the whole world hope of a better tomorrow.

Hope is a wonderful and infectious thing and the recovery of the world economy was accelerated as people began to believe in what they were doing again. They actually believed that the governments of the world had done something to help them and build a better future for them and their children. The President's advisors spoke to him daily about the newfound growth of the American economy and congratulated him on his brave decision to build the fair and cease military action. The forecast was that before the show ended that employment would be at its highest in many years and would present huge financial benefits for the country.

The President was stood in his favourite spot, right on top of the sky ride south tower, when the show opened. He watched in amazement at the opening ceremony and couldn't help but feel some pride for his and Marshalls fair. He knew he couldn't have done this without Marshall and the incredible dedication of the thousands of workers that had built this big, beautiful display. It was Marshalls ideas that had lifted the designs off the pages and built the many displays.

As he stood atop the towering construction he couldn't help but notice the fantastic aerial which stood some hundred feet above him. The tip of the aerial shone in a fantastic blue, which bathed the area in light it didn't appear to be just a decoration and mesmerised everyone who looked upon it. He smiled to himself and thought this was a fantastic detail and showed the level of quality that his people had bestowed upon this fair. As he looked down over the displays he could see that everyone was in a state of euphoria at the incredible and life changing inventions that were on offer. Every man, woman and child that was visiting the fair were smiling and having fun. He felt proud of himself and the achievements of his country.

The view from space was good as well. Frank Farley was looking on with pride and let Marshall know that it was incredible to finally see mankind rejoicing together in perfect peace and in awe at its ability to invent. The most important thing to Frank was that everything was ready and a launch date was to be set. He informed Marshall that the perfect alignment of the stars would be on the 29th March 2022 and he would organise the launch from his planet and just seventy-two minutes later the car would land on Earth, onto the sky ride which was built perfectly and was transmitting correctly.

Marshall's mobile telephone rang in his hand as he looked down on the hundreds of people vying to gain access to the fair.

He casually pressed the green button on the keypad and lifted the device to his ear,

"Hello Frank" he said, acting as if everyone received interstellar phone calls on a daily basis.

"Hello Marshall, you have developed the fair perfectly to plan and we would like to congratulate you in building the only receiver that will work perfectly and finally link our glorious civilisations forever!" barked Frank as he failed miserably to control his excitement at finally achieving his biggest dream.

"What is the plan from here?" asked Marshall.

"Well next we will set the date for the transmission and decide between us what we have to do to get mankind to see us arrive in all our glory and offer galactic friendship!" answered Frank.

"When will it be?"

"We have set the date for the 29th March 2022. The stars are perfectly aligned for that date and we will link forever! Before transmission we will announce to the Earth that we are arriving and this way your scheming politicians will have no say on who knows we exist"

Marshall felt a cold shiver go down his spine as Franks last statement bounced around his brain like a rubber ball on a squash court. He didn't know how the public and politicians were going to react. All he knew was that he was going to be the focus of a lot of attention and he needed to keep this secret for a little longer.

The fair continued for two years at an incredible pace with over two million people attending each year and a sustained growth in global interest the fair could only be termed as a runaway success. The ongoing effects of this display of mankind's talent were measurable in many ways and not least by not only the recovery of the economy but the reawakening of mans desire to achieve something better. A belief that tomorrow did not need to be the same as today, that we could leave a better place for our children and live in peace.

One of the biggest benefits to mankind was the reopening of the space programme that would see the government declaring a desire to set up bases on the moon and finally send astronauts to Mars. The Stromberg Institute had provided, with a little help from the others, a new type of propulsion system that would increase the speed of spacecraft ten fold. This would have the effect of allowing man to reach his nearest neighbours in a fraction of the time it would take with conventional rockets. The moon would be twelve hours away and mars little more than a week of travel. This technology had finally allowed mankind to start to fulfil their need to expand.

The reopening of the space programme made Marshall smile more than any other development. He had provided them with the greatest leaps forward since the original moon landings but the technology contained in the Skyride would, to a degree, make these new faster space vehicles redundant. The Skyride could effectively be tuned to access many different locations and in theory once man had built receivers on these other planets then they would be no further away, in travelling time, than the local store. Mankind could populate the universe within a few years as they could spread out and build bases all over the immediate Solar System and beyond. The technology that was now available would enable the building of airtight, usable buildings on Martian soil which would be able to sustain life and present, for the first time in mankind's history, permanent and liveable buildings away from Earths protective atmosphere. In one of his many conversations with Frank he had been told of a machine, which was being developed, which when activated would be able to turn most suitable planets into an environment which could sustain human life. Marshall had never seen this device but he was sure that if Frank said it then at some stage he would develop it.

Marshall stood staring into space as his mind wandered onto another plain of consciousness that allowed him to build and plan dreams like they were ideas being thrown around on a computer screen. This was his only gift off Frank and had happened one night when he was soundly sleeping. Frank had just opened the channels of his brain that allowed Marshall to think more clearly. Everyone had the ability to do this but we just hadn't developed it.

During this planning he realised again that he was the only person on the planet that knew what was coming, and it wasn't going to very long before the whole of civilisation knew what had been happening for hundreds of years.

Petrol

"Find me something in that bloody stuff that used to come through space" barked a more than angry President to a room of scientists who were busy looking at many different ideas that could be used to reduce the pollution that man was throwing into the air every minute of every day.

Since the early eighties the pressure on the world's powers from the United Nations to reduce their emissions had become palpable. The President of America was under an incredible amount of pressure to reduce the ecological impact her country was making on the environment.

"There must be something in there we can make use of!" she shouted as her eager advisers looked through the many dog-eared documents that had been read and re-read since they had been communicated through the stars over many years.

"I think I may have found something!" shouted a small portly man who was working at a brightly lit desk at the back of the darkened room.

The other advisers in the room gasped in anticipation as he stood and walked nervously towards the waiting President. They knew that although some fantastic discoveries had been made in the paperwork, many scientists and professors had been led on a fool's errand by what looked like a fantastic clue. They also knew that the President was very unforgiving of claims that could change the world, and the subsequent effect on the advisers would be that they would be shown the door along with their useless developments. The Presidents advisers would then ensure that their tattered reputation would not allow them any further employment within the scientific field.

As the nervous adviser reached the President he started to talk whilst furtively looked around the room for any signs of support from his silent colleagues.

"I think I have found a new type of cleaner fuel" he stuttered as the President glowered at him.

"I have heard this a thousand times, and a thousand times I have told the fool involved that the oil companies will not allow it!" barked the President as she showed little regard for the advisers incredible discovery. The thinking behind this outburst from the President was that the last adviser to breech the subject of fuel had indeed found the cleanest and most readily available fuel on the planet.

Water.

The others had discovered years ago that by a simple process they could get the hydrogen out of rainwater with a device that not only was simple but also was massively efficient, and more importantly totally harmless to the environment.
Unfortunately when the old President presented this to the Oil Companies, he was ridiculed and questioned on his sanity. This was mainly because the discovery would effectively end the need for expensive oil. On Earth crude oil is worth billions of dollars to its shareholders and the world economy. On top of this how could any government tax water that fell from the sky for free! The workingman could collect it himself and drive around with no taxation! That idea was killed off nearly as quickly as the man who found it in the paperwork. One of the big oil companies immediately paid many millions of dollars to the election fund that year just to take that paperwork away. The idea, like so many before it, was locked away and, with the exception of a few rumours, effectively forgotten.

"Don't worry Miss, its not going to effect our wonderful oil industry in fact it will, for the first time in years, make them look good!" continued the now excited adviser.

"How on earth could any invention possibly make them look good?" asked a puzzled looking President.

"It is a very simple process that the others did in their very early years of transport when they too still relied on fossil fuels. They also realised that by burning fuel you create pollution. The pollution would eventually cause other environmental problems and so they developed this!"

He thrust the paperwork towards the Presidents outstretched hand before commencing a detailed description of the multitude of scribbled notes on the crumpled paper.

"It's a very inexpensive and efficient way of taking the lead pollutant out of petrol!" continued a now very excited adviser.

"We could sell it to the public as a great environment saver with added health benefits. We could also charge more for the privilege of using it, even though it is considerably cheaper to produce. The garages and motor companies could be told to needlessly alter existing cars, at great cost, to use it! It's a win win situation!" he exclaimed.

The President quickly analysed the situation as for once something seemed too good to be true. The maths were easy as it will be more expensive which equals more tax, more work for garages equals more income tax, more needless technology on new and used cars equals more tax!

"Well you're the inventor would you like to call it?" shouted out a now excited President, who had rapidly figured out that this a great money spinning idea with environmental benefits and was also an election winner.

"I would like to call it new clean fuel," said the now rising adviser, who was looking around the room at his smiling colleagues with a new found air of authority. He could already feel the pride of a promotion coming his way before his brief daydream was abruptly cut short.

"Don't be foolish! That is a truly stupid name!" barked the President as she quickly knocked him off his pedestal, much to the delight of his envious colleagues. After a brief conversation with one of her faceless advisers, who always appeared to be glued to her ear with his incessant whispering, she stood and made an announcement:

" I have decided that we will release details of it under the name 'Unleaded fuel' "

She ushered the cowering adviser away with some contempt after blatantly renaming his discovery to suit her own political needs. This was sadly not what she wanted to do, nor what the adviser deserved, but merely a necessary political procedure. She was sure that this vastly intelligent little man had a full and meaningful life outside the walls of the establishment. What he didn't know was that he was now in a very exclusive and elite club of people on earth who had made incredible discoveries but would never get any reward or public recognition.

He also wasn't to know it but he was now living his last day on Earth.

The saddest fact about working with the others transmissions was that you quickly became a liability to any government and a risk that they would not be willing to take. If you went to the media and disclosed facts from these papers then you could quickly convince people to ask difficult questions. The answers to these questions would be made a whole lot more difficult if details of the others were also disclosed at the same time. Unfortunately, in line with government directives, the people who made discoveries based on alien designs had an uncanny knack of dying or disappearing not long afterwards.

That night he left work convinced he had finally been put forward for promotion after many years of dedicated service. As he carefully drove his car home to tell his wife and two young children what an incredible thing he had done at work that day, he had a terrible, unexplained traffic accident that cost him his life.

His legacy was the discovery of a cleaner fuel that would save countless species on Earth and prevent massive amounts of environmental damage. Unfortunately, this has had been the case for centuries and countless people before him, no one would ever know his name.

Chapter 14.

The Announcement.

On the morning of 29th March 2022 Marshall awoke with butterflies in his stomach. He knew today would alter all of mankind's belief and the futures of all living beings here on Earth.

The machines were ready. Marshall was ready. He hoped the World was ready.

On the day the sky ride was closed to the general public due to necessary repairs, this of course was a cover for the landing that was due on this day. Marshall was in constant communication with Frank Farley via a mobile link, which he had developed by altering the signal on his mobile phone, a development that had even impressed Frank himself. The orders were simple: ensure the sky ride is set with both cars on the east side at the desired time. The space ship would land on the rails as if it was always there and would coast to a halt at the western tower. The only thing that concerned Frank was the heat that would be developed, this he had combated by placing a new covering on the spacecraft made of a heat-reducing polymer. A polymer thought of by a toddler who burnt his hand on his dad's teacup, just another dazzling example of the sleep schools.

Marshall confirmed everything was in place and waited.

Whilst he waited he thought of all the time that he had spent with the professor and all the time behind the fence. He also thought of his parents and how they had supported him during his developing years and never questioned his bizarre behaviour. When he was a teenager he would disappear for days on end and no one ever knew where he was. He would of course be behind the fence with the professor, working on various projects and learning all about the others.

He sat and looked down over the Worlds Fair. A fair, which had been his responsibility for the last five years and to the rest of mankind, it would be apparent why he wanted everything correct. The people on the ground would have no idea what was happening today and what would happen after this day. In a few short hours the Earth would be an entirely different place as man finally accepted that he was not alone in the universe. Marshall caught himself breaking into a cold sweat as he just really hoped that mankind was ready.

At exactly ten o clock in the evening his mobile phone sparked into life. Frank Farley shouted down the phone, with the excitement of a five-year-old opening presents on Christmas morning, that they had launched the pod from their planet. The one thing that Marshall had never quite got used to was that, his friend Frank Farley would ring him like he was just around the corner but in reality he was light years away on a planet that was pretty much identical to ours. He had only asked Frank about how the link worked once and the rather abrupt answer that he got was 'Its highly developed technology, we know how it all works! One day we may impart the plans.' a polite way of saying that Marshalls underdeveloped brain wouldn't understand, even if Frank tried his best to explain.

Marshall felt sick to the stomach, as he now knew that the events that followed would be out of his control and he just hoped that the President would understand what he had done. Over the last few years he had misled everyone, he alone knew what was planned all along and he suddenly had an over-whelming desire to share the information. He had told no one and he suddenly felt very alone.

Marshall picked up his mobile phone and rang the only person alive who would know the answers.

"Frank, I am scared." Marshall whimpered into the phone as he suddenly felt like the little boy who was stood at the top of the bank, on the cinder path, staring at the gap in the fence all those years ago.

"Marshall" replied Frank, "of course you are, I would be if I was in your position as well, but just think of all the years we have talked. You know that this is going to benefit all of mankind. You alone will be the reason that Earth finally came out of that dark corner of your Solar System and joined us. We will cure all your diseases, open up your minds and show you how to develop further than you could have dreamed."

"You wouldn't be human if you weren't nervous" added Frank as the connection was disrupted as the signal crackled and was lost.

As the signal died Marshall looked towards the western tower of the Skyride as the blue beacon shone brighter than the sun. It had been exactly seventy-two minutes since that first call from Frank and now the arrival of the pod was imminent. Marshall was now very much in unchartered territory and could only hope that all would become clearer as he watched along with the all other attendees of the fair and the world's population. The bright blue light bathed the entire area in an eerie light that made the shadows in doorways appear darker than night. The night sky suddenly lit with the crackles of static electricity as the cameras of the world's news networks instantly trained their gaze onto the Skyride.

Marshall watched as the electricity to all the other parts of the show slowly failed and the cables surrounding the beacon glowed with the incredible heat of the transmission.

It was time.

Marshall knew that the events of the next few minutes would irreversibly change the face of human history, as mankind would finally know for definite that they were not alone. The only grace would be that these were not ugly evil aliens that had been portrayed in every Hollywood space movie ever, but were just like us in appearance and wanted, more than anything, to be friends. Marshall had often been told by the Professor over the years that when the truth came out about the contact over the years, and the politician's manipulation of the inventions, then there would be a lot of questions asked of those in power. The Professor always hoped that there would be survivors from the original contact that would be bought to justice for their total and absolute guilt at the misuse of the many fantastic gifts.

Slowly the blue beacon of light gave way to a bright red apparition, which appeared to be changing shape as it slowly jittered into position under the cables of the east tower as the crowds watched in awe. The people on the fairground began to shout and cheer as the light show continued, perhaps thinking it was just another fantastic show for them to enjoy. The whole area was bathed in red light and a shattering blast of static electricity made everyone's hair stand on end as the craft landed.

The craft slid slowly down the cables towards the west tower it was bathed in an orange afterglow as the heat emitted from it like a giant radiator. The flurry of excitement continued within the crowds every television screen at the fair and all over the globe sparked into life. After the initial static burst of life on the screen a short test transmission screen appeared and within a minute this clearing there, in front of every person on Earth, on the television was Frank Farley. He spoke slowly as he gave the citizens of Earth his first message:

"Hello Earth this is Frank Farley II. I am from the Nebulus planet on the far side of the Galaxy.

Some of you, from our contact over the years, will already know me but sadly most of you will not. We have been in contact for many years and unbeknownst to most of you the technology you take for granted was probably of our design.

We are friends and we want to help the people of Earth to develop and fulfil your own potential.

With the help of Marshall, we have sent you our first ship full of technology that will provide the tools to change forever yourselves and your planet. We are not the enemy. We are just like you but our planet has not been ravaged by greed and war like yours has. Since our original contact in your Victorian times, successive governments have kept the technology for themselves. We wanted to help you all but a select few were more interested in building weapons. In a similar amount of history to yours we have explored the Galaxy and fulfilled our potential.

You are not, and never have been, alone.

We now have, via the Skyride, a link between the planets. The cars can be used to transport people, computers and ideas. We sincerely hope that the whole planet finally accepts our hand of friendship.

We have sent instructions on how to use the technology and what to do next. We look forward to finally getting to know you all and helping you all to become better people."

Upon finishing his speech the screens blinked to darkness rapidly followed by the shining blue beacon. The world looked on in silence as the still glowing car continued to slide slowly and deliberately towards the Western tower.

The President was in the oval office when the announcement was made. He slumped back in his chair and awaited the onslaught of questions from all around the globe. He knew that this was his fair and everyone would want to know what was going on.

He reached for the phone and rang Marshall. He needed answers and he needed them now. Marshall casually picked up the phone and spoke immediately.

"Hello Mr President I thought you might call" said a calm Marshall,

"What the hell is going on? You have misled me! I need answers now!" shouted the President as he stood and held the phone like his life depended on it.

"I knew this would be a shock but let me explain." before Marshall could even get the words out the President was already asking more questions.

"Shock!" He yelled as the advisers in the office looked on, "We have got bloody Aliens talking to the world and I instigated it! You're not wrong it's a shock what the hell is going on and who the hell are they?" screamed an angry and confused President.

Marshall thought about what to say next before replying,

"They are friendly and have been talking to me since I was a child. The original site where this whole thing was planned from is in Swadlincote. I found it as a child and the Professor, who lived there, taught me everything. He also told me what your successive governments have done with the technology we have been given. The others would not risk giving their ideas to a select few again so when they had the chance to speak to everyone we took it. You gave us that chance and for that you will always be remembered as the President who finally lifted the lid on hundreds of years of lies"

"I don't want to be that Marshall!" replied the President before slamming down the phone in a fit of rage brought on by his impression that he had been corralled into an idea which suddenly seemed out of his control from the start.

The President slumped back in his chair again. The various telephones, representing all the departments of his government, on his desk had started ringing and he knew he needed answers before he spoke to anyone.

He picked up the telephone and hit the redial button.

"Marshall I need answers this is too big for any of us, people are wanting to know what's happening, they want to know what's going to happen to Earth" spoke a suddenly calmer and more lucid President who had realised that Marshall was the one inhabitant of Earth who now knew what was going on.

Marshall thought for a moment and continued his conversation,

"They are our friends. They have tried to land here before and your predecessors' all knew about it. They hid the technology and treated the others with contempt. The nuclear bomb! The missile! The rocket! The computer! Spaceflight, engines, telephones, satellites, television. The list is endless and it was all their technology given to all of us to utilise in a peaceful way, except successive governments used it to their own benefit. They sometimes even built the transmitters wrong in order to just get the ideas. The atom bomb should have been a power station providing free energy that would provide benefits for all of us! Television is an educational device that would make professors out of us all! Even unleaded fuel was their idea!"

Marshall had one chance to get this through and he knew it.

" We knew if we let you all know then this would have been hidden, just like every other time. You would have hid the truth from the population of earth and used the inventions for ever more elaborate weapons. It's the very reason they stopped coming here all those years ago. Well the Professor told me what to do and I did it. I have bought the truth to the masses!" Marshall said as he stood back and watched the rapidly approaching car across the steel cables.

The President looked around the room. Nearly every adviser he had was in the Oval Office and they had all heard the telephone conversation. He put down the phone and spoke;

"What do we do next Gentlemen?" asked the President who was sat with his elbows on the desk cupping his head in his hands.

"We deny the whole thing as a hoax." Presented the head of the CIA as if he knew what to do instantly.

He continued, "an elaborate hoax conducted by a select few, just like Roswell…"

The President looked up "What do you mean?"

"Like Roswell. The bloody Aliens have been bothering us for years! They want to come here and take away all our luxuries and promote the need for everyone to have a say. We cannot run a country like that! Religion would collapse and more importantly what about the shareholders!"

"So this is all true then?" questioned a now confused President.

"Yes its true. They have been trying to get in touch with us since The Victorian days when they asked the English to build the Crystal Palace in London. They couldn't get it right and kept burning things down. They would apologise and send us some plans for machines. Some of it was unreadable but some bits were brilliant! We built the nuke off those plans and you cannot deny that has earnt us a lot of money and respect over the years!" answered the grey haired old man who the President couldn't remember seeing before.

"An alien race has been talking to us for all these years and no one bothered to tell me?" screamed a now angry President.

"Well.." started the CIA agent, "They haven't spoke to us since we built the nuke. They said it was not what they wanted us to do. They wanted to build a bloody power station with free electric for everyone! The shareholders would never agree to that"

The President sat back down and looked around. He thought to himself for a moment 'How had this happened?', 'What was he thinking letting this young Marshall fellow run a massive show without question or monetary restraint'. He could get voted out over this he thought as his head stopped spinning in a moment of clarity. He spent a few moments considering his options as he stared out the window at the already growing crowds at the fence of the White House. He slowly turned and addressed the room:

"Destroy it!" barked the president, "destroy it now!" he shouted at the generals.

Chapter 15

Franks Reaction.

Frank wasn't at all shocked by Earth's immature and violent response to his message of friendship. His people had asked him to form a link with the people of Earth, but had made it quite clear that this would be for a final time. He knew that he would have to report to his people that the Earthlings had responded in their usual violent way. With this presumed outcome in mind the others had discussed a number of options that were open to them at this time and all of these would be devastating to the people of Earth, and also completely out of Frank's hands. The others would decide Earths fate as a true democracy after all the options had been investigated.

Their technology was so far ahead of Earths that a number of devastating events could be unleashed or alternatively they could decide to literally sit back and let mankind rot in its own anger and self-importance. This would probably be better than all other choices, in Frank's opinion, as people of Earth would have to sit there and forever wonder what could have been and also would the others ever come back. They could waste the rest of their miserable lives looking at the skies and building ever more futile weapons to hurt each other with.

After much deliberation the others decided to vote on the two most plausible options that were open to them. The first, and most controversial choice was to use a long-range plasma bolt to move Earth slightly out of its delicate orbit and thus changing what life it would be able to sustain. The second choice was less dramatic but just as dangerous. This would involve the use of the mindblast technology in the removal of mans knowledge of all the inventions and technologies that the others had ever given to them.

The others had historically never been war mongering or aggressive people so the thought of 'nudging' the planet out of orbit and killing billions of innocent people sat rather uneasily on their palette, however, the thought of reclaiming all the technologies that the earthlings had used to ill effect had gained a substantial vote amongst the people. Their main reasons seemed to be that these were their ideas, thought of by the people for the people, to develop their planet and improve everyone's lifestyles. The various links over the years had allowed the people of Earth to share in these developments and have the opportunity to improve their lives. However, the various governments on Earth had used these great ideas and developments for weapons. The others had extended the hand of friendship and it had been bitten time and again, and in their collective view this was totally unacceptable.

The others passed the vote on the second option and then turned to Frank and his department for the solution of this dilemma. The people knew what they wanted to do and Frank was duty bound to provide the required service. Frank sat and pleaded with the collective people of his planet to give the earthlings another chance but his pleas were rebuffed. How could he remove knowledge from Earth? It was against his principals but he knew that if that's what the people wanted then that was his job he had to do it whether he agreed or not.

After much deliberation by Frank's team and his final pleas for mercy he reluctantly opened the safe and unlocked the high security cage containing the 'Mindblast' machine. Even though he had quite recently used this machine to good effect, he had always hated the concept of messing with people's minds totally against their will.

His team spent some development time on research and after a few successful trials they reset the machine to total removal and connected it to the transmitter, which pointed straight at the huge receiver behind the fence. This would receive the signal and transmit a global blanket of energy that would remove mankind's knowledge of every idea that had been transmitted over the years.

With tears in his eyes and with a heavy heart Frank fired up the machine up for one last time and reluctantly reached forward to press the button.

At this moment he thought of the great people he had spoke to over the years and the dreamers that still lived on the planet that his people had become so obsessed with over the years. Going right back to Prince there had always been someone prepared to listen and he couldn't help but feel a little guilty at his part in sending Earth all these great ideas that they had no idea what to do with. He couldn't help but feel sorry for the pathetic creatures.

In a moment of contemplation he thought of all the fantastic inventions and monuments that had been jointly developed between the two planets. It all started with the Crystal Palace, then followed onto the Eiffel Tower, the Statue of Liberty, the debacle in Suffolk, the atom in Brussels and his own personal favourite, and the only working model, the original Skyride in Chicago. They were so very close in 1933 and he just wished that he had got it right the first time as the human race was so much more open minded in those early years of the 20th century and not cynical at any new ideas. As tears filled his eyes he regretted the day that he had sent the plans for the nuclear reactor that the researchers on Earth had turned into the most destructive bomb in the universe. He also rued the day that man started looking inwards at themselves and stopped reaching out to the stars. He thought how his people had helped to put man on the moon and then man had become more obsessed with the latest ring tone rather than reaching further out into the universe. It always seemed to his people that if a person on Earth tried to develop new ideas they would be ridiculed long before their developments were embraced. They would often discuss and be amused by mans apparent resistance to computer technology before it finally became mainstream and also their total and absolute dependence on burning fossil fuels. All man ever had to do was embrace the power of the planet, like his distant relatives, and all the free energy they could ever need was there already. They burnt the records of the past and they had no idea on how to discover it again in the future. The one unique thing that amused the others the most about mankind was there total and absolute worship of currency. Money was the god to all men. A persons success is not measured in inventions or abilities just cold hard money, for if you are not rich then there is no way you are successful. Mankind had achieved star status in becoming the only species in the entire universe to enslave itself to printed pieces of paper and discs of precious metals.

As the tears rolled down his face he realised that his determination to link with Earth had just been a lifelong folly of epic proportions.

"I have wasted large chunks of my life trying to form a link and it was all for nothing." He shouted into the empty room in his last cry on anguish before he finally composed himself. He fleetingly thought of using the mindblast on himself to erase any thoughts, or memories, of the ridiculous blue green planet people once and for all.

Then he thought of Marshall.

This young man had been mentored to help construct the link all of his life. He had blindly believed in everything that he had been told, he was the only one brave enough to look behind the fence and he had nearly single handed built the incredible Worlds Fair that had finally presented to mankind a working link between the planets. He had manipulated the President and the population to believe in better and to turn their back on war and start to build a better future. Most important of all he had convinced Franks people to try again. To once again try and link with Earth and build a better future for all of mankind. Those very men had let Marshall down as much as they had let down Frank and the others.

Marshall was too good to be left to live in a cave and learn how to make fire again, he deserved better treatment for his efforts and the memory of the Professor deserved more respect as well.

Frank immediately summoned a news conference for the people.

The news conference took the appearance of a global news flash. This had to happen because the people were expecting immediate action against Earth, but Frank wanted a vote on Marshall. He put forward his argument for discussion and waited for the answer.

The people of Franks planet didn't need to vote in kiosks or by post as their mind had rapidly become one in the development of their educational systems. All the individual had to do was tune their brain into the global network and they could access any information or attend any meeting in the world. The decisions of the people were made into law immediately and everyone had a voice. The only over-riding written law of the Planet was that everyone whether they are a man, woman and child must agree or it was never to be a law.

Frank had raised an interesting issue and the people of the world listened.

A decision was made and, via mindblast, a message was sent to Earth.

After this Frank reprogrammed to computers to facilitate total removal and fired the Mindblast at Earth on full power. The receiver in Swadlincote instantly received the message was blasted through the atmosphere into the brain of every living person on Earth.

The total removal was instant and completely devastating.

Chapter 16

Departure and delivery

Marshall was stood motionless staring at the Skyride as the chaos spun around him. He now knew that the world wasn't ready for the aliens to talk to them as friends. Over two hundred years of Hollywood had convinced them that all aliens were evil. The people thought Frank was evil and the others were going to invade Earth and destroy them.

As Marshall stood staring up at his wonderful creation he was unaware that little more than a hundred miles away two jet fighters had been scrambled and were taking off with the sole purpose of destroying the skyride and forever breaking the link with the alien nation. The President had ordered complete destruction of the Worlds Fair and had already instructed the police to evacuate it and to arrest Marshall. The truth was that the President really didn't care if Marshall survived or not, he had broken so many laws that his life was going to be worthless when the courts had finished sentencing him. The public would certainly be calling for his head after he had exposed their planet to the aliens.

The President certainly felt that Marshall had deserted them and misled him all along. He had not only misled him he had also misled the country and the President had to be seen by his people to be taking decisive action. His predecessors' had always shown an iron fist when faced with a possible invasion or threat to the shores of his great nation and he would do the same. He would show America's military might by completely destroying the very source of the problem. By doing this he could once and for all show his people that he was a great leader who had stopped an alien race from invading our shores. The people would still demand answers and the shareholders would demand to know why they had lost money on this ridiculous and dangerous folly.

The aliens would cost them money and the President knew if he was to stand any chance of getting through this then he would need the backing of the financial institutions. He was now all to aware that the people who had ran these companies for many years had known of the others all along and based most their business on this brilliant but mostly misused technology. If the public found out the complete truth then many companies would be financially ruined. He could not risk this.

The President looked around the oval office and wondered how on Earth he had got himself into this crazy situation, he had risked everything on this folly and now he was going to be the only leader in American history to bomb his own country to destroy something! If he arrested Marshall then he could scapegoat the young professor into taking the blame, for performing a dangerous hoax that had risked national security. He could go further than that, he thought, he could say that Marshall was in league with some terrorist corporation and the Skyride was in fact an incredible type of bomb that would have killed millions! He would be a hero for averting the disaster and destroying it before it could be used. A show of strength was obviously the answer so he called his military commanders and one by one ordered the re-commencement of military activity globally to present the impression to his people that they were under threat. The war machine rolled out in all the countries where peace had been so successful and the cold dark grip of fear began to embrace the Earth again.

Marshall moved towards the skyride and, against the flow of people, started to ascend the western tower towards the cars. He climbed the steps and looked around at mans last hope of building something good disappearing before him. The avenues below him started to echo with sounds of crime as the beautiful atmosphere of freedom rapidly descended into heartbreak and despair. The noise made him weep with anger as he heard the horrific noise of the police firing on their own people in order to try and resume order.

He felt like he had caused this and the feeling of guilt was unbearable as he climbed the stairs and entered the eastbound car. He slowly closed and locked the door before throwing himself down into the luxury reclined leatherette seats of the space car. The sound proofed interior of the car provided him with a welcome escape from reality where he thought he could sit and wait for his own unenviable fate at the hands of the trigger-happy police officers. He knew, from his dealings with the government, that he would be scapegoated into taking the full responsibility for the terrible events that had followed the announcement.

He closed his eyes and for a moment wished all those many years ago in the pub garden that he had never gone behind the fence. He thought of the Professor and those who had been close to him as he grew up. He also thought of the many hundreds of people he had lied to in order to build his dream. In a rare moment of peace in the anarchy that had engulfed the globe he fruitlessly looked to the heavens and began to ask for forgiveness.

This moment of peace and tranquillity was suddenly and inexplicably disturbed with a massive jolt as the car started to move along the cables toward the east tower.

Marshall sat riveted to the chair; his eyes wide open in fear, as the space car slowly began accelerating down the cables. In a state of panic Marshall looked out of the window to try and assess what was going on. In the distance he could see two jet fighters dramatically swooping through the skyscrapers of Chicago as the pilots followed there misplaced orders and locked onto their target. The missiles locked onto their target and prepared to launch towards the very place where Marshall was sitting. Marshall could see the missiles launch and froze into the warm enveloping seat and closed his eyes tightly as he said goodbye to Earth and tried not to contemplate his impending doom. Whilst his eyes were closed he thought of his mum and dad who had held his hand as a child and as he grew up had never stopped helping him to achieve his dreams, he imagined how they would feel if they had seen him now? He couldn't decide if they would be proud of him or they would have been in total dismay at the lies that had seen him in this position. He consoled himself by believing that soon he would know, as he would be with them again.

Marshall sat with his eyes closed tightly shut and his hands tensely gripping the leatherette seat he awaited the impending explosion and the end of his eventful life. His eyes were closed for what seemed like an eternity.

Whilst Marshall was sat awaiting his fate one thousand light years away Frank Farley announced his impending retirement from public service. As he finished his brief but emotional speech he asked for forgiveness for his actions and fired the mindblast at Earth for one last time. It had been agreed that after this the Mindblast would be destroyed and all public knowledge of the machine would be erased from the records. Frank would find a worthy successor and just as his boss had done all those many years ago he would slowly slip from the public eye.

Marshall waited and after a short time he opened his eyes and slowly turned his head to look out of the window. The planes were gone and the city was in total darkness. As he peered out of the window in total disbelief he could make out the outline of two parachuting pilots slowly drifting down towards the ground. As looked on in amazement his gaze lowered to the avenues of the fair where he could see that the people had stopped fighting and were just wandering around as if in a daze. There were no lights on the streets and no noise from the police sirens. The sound of modern life had stopped like someone hitting snooze on his or her noisy and annoying alarm clock.

Although Marshall was totally unaware of what had happened to Earth he was actually the sole person to come out the mindblast intact. Frank had programmed the mindblast to remove all knowledge of any alien invention from everyone on the planet except one person, who would be safely insulated within the car on the Skyride. Marshall would have the honour of being the sole representative for what Earth could have achieved had it followed the correct path of progress through all these years.

The car began to rapidly accelerate along the cables and as it did the window shutters came down.

"Oh my god!" shouted Marshall as the loud roar of the hyperactive side drives fired up. The whole car shook for a second before the multi-dimensional drives let out an ear-shattering explosion that would envy any war machine. The car accelerated harshly, pinning Marshall to his padded seat before he passed out. The confused people of Chicago saw a white flash of lightening and the car lurched forward at an incredible speed. The people, dazed and confused, looked up towards the skyride as the car gave out yet another ear shattering bang and appeared to burst into flame. The aerial at the top of the tower shone bright blue and within the next heartbeat the car completely disappeared. The cables were still alight and some arcs of static electricity hummed around the towers presenting the last artificial light on the planet.

Marshall awoke still in his seat and hung onto his seatbelt as the car lurched from side to side. The temperature in the cabin had increased alarmingly and Marshall felt the first beads of sweat forming on his balding head. He reached into the inside pocket of his jacket and he pulled out the pictures of everyone who had ever been close to him and hoped they would forgive him for his follies. The heat increased until Marshall was finding hard to breath but as quickly as the thought entered his head a huge gust of cold air swept around him like the waves washing around a rock on a beach. He suddenly remembered the cooling system built into every car and thanked the engineers for building it perfectly to the design.

After half of an hour Marshall plucked up the courage to get out of his seat and stand in the central aisle. He started to walk forward to the communication screen at the front of the cabin. He slowly and clumsily reached forward to activate the device to operate the cameras outside of the car. Although he knew he could not steer the car he just wanted to see where he was going just like he had done in his dads van, by standing on the back seat, all those many years ago.

Just as his fingertips touched the perfectly engineered controls the car abruptly stopped.

The resulting force swept Marshall off his feet and sent him crashing into the screens at the front of the ship. As he lay feeling sorry for himself and assessing his wounds his eyes were drawn across to the windows. The shutters were lifting and letting in brilliant sunlight that not only stung his eyes but lit the inside of the gold cabin like a Chinese lantern. He started to get the all too familiar feeling of an impending doom as he could make out the shapes of figures silhouetted in the sunlight and they were looking in on him. He considered the fact that he had probably broken every law in the rulebook and the American authorities would have no hesitation in locking him up for a very long time.

The door let out a loud hiss and slowly opened. The warm air flooded the cabin and Marshall looked on as a familiar looking old man stood looking at him, his ruffled figure standing out from the brilliant deep blue sky behind him. The old man slowly raised his hand and started to wave and spoke very slowly:

"Hello Marshall and welcome to the stars"

Marshall immediately recognised the old man in the doorway as Frank Farley and as his head slowly clicked back into gear he realised that he was no longer on Earth. He had travelled across space to the other planet. The Skyride had worked exactly as planned and it had transported Marshall safely to the other planet.

Meanwhile back on Earth amongst all the chaos that had ensued, since the transmission, no one noticed the door of the incoming craft slowly opening. With some trepidation a young man stepped onto the alien planet and rubbed his eyes. He looked around and took in the ensuing scenes of chaos and disorder. Shaking his head in disbelief he slowly reached back inside the craft and grabbed two large suitcases. He carefully carried the cases as he walked around the loading bay. Upon locating the staircase he turned take one last look around at the skyline before he descended the steel staircase. He opened and exited the fire door at the foot of the east tower and walked around to the control centre. He opened the door and slowly entered the safe room before locking the door behind him.

Upon settling in the centre he opened the suitcases, which contained what appeared to be computer parts, and slowly connected the contents together with various coloured wires. After switching the machine on he raised his hand and looked at the small screen on his wristwatch as it sparked into life. He touched the screen three times and began to speak:

"Nebulus, Earth base has been connected and secured, the skyride is safe"; he continued.

"I await further instructions, this is the Professor."

Chapter 17

Looking sideways at Home

The people of Frank's planet decided by a majority that something would have to be done about Earth. The fact that nearly all of their gifts had been used for war had finally made them realise that mankind could not be trusted with the technology, and the only way to reclaim it would be via 'mindblast'.

The others had now demanded that the machine should be used, for one last time, to effectively wipe the slate clean and remove mankind's knowledge of all the technology that had been gifted to them over the centuries. As Frank stood hovering over the machine he realised that once mankind's brains had been cleared of the knowledge there would be no going back, all of mankind would suffer for the sake of the few that demanded weapons and power. The greed of the generations that had mis-used the ideas had effectively sentenced the good people of earth to centuries of strife as they would have to start again, these facts alone made Frank a very sad old man. Frank's love of mankind and Earth had now stretched back over two centuries and he could not believe it was to come to this bitter end. The only saving grace was that Marshall was now safe in the insulated interior of the spacecraft and would soon be on his way to a better future. With the thought of Marshall and the Professor still clear in his head Frank reached forward and pressed the erase button on the mindblast machine.

The biggest problem that came from activating the machine was that Frank, nor any other living person, had any idea how this would affect the planet earth or the people living on it. The others understood that all technology would stop working and the very concept of it would become alien to mans conscious state but how this would pan out over the next few days and months was a mystery to them all. The effects on society would surely be devastating but not nearly as bad as some of the weapons that man had made, from their great ideas, over the years. They would still be able to hunt and feed themselves, which, thought Frank, was roughly where mankind was when they first started to get involved all those many centuries ago.

The real effect on the people of Earth was immediate and devastating. Any machine or gadget that contained any trace of alien technology stopped working immediately and mankind suffered a collective temporary blackout as their brains effectively rebooted with no knowledge of the machines around them. All public services ceased to work and over the first few hours there were many disasters around the globe, as the planes fell from the skies and nuclear power stations, unable to shutdown automatically, failed and resulted in multiple devastating meltdowns. All transport systems ceased to work and most importantly for the others was that every weapon ever made became no more than useless lumps of metal.

By far the most devastating effect was on individual human beings as their brains were immediately reprogrammed to have no knowledge of any technology that had ever been given. Suddenly and quite dramatically the whole human race stopped being able to use computers, drive cars, pilot planes and most importantly understand what had happened. The result was agonising cries of anguish from all over the globe as confusion rapidly turned into fear and panic. Those who could returned to their homes, which were unlit and without water, to be with their loved ones and try to figure out what to do next and how to survive within this now hospitable environment.

Stone Age man was now effectively stood in the centre of modern industrial cities.

What followed over the next few months was a total breakdown of society, as mankind tried but failed to survive without the others advanced technology. The old shells of factories quickly became caves and wildlife ran amok reclaiming everything that man had decimated during his rule of the planet. Mother nature had been subjected to the destructive power of man for many years and now it was time for her to reclaim the planet. The population of Earth slowly dwindled down to an eco sustainable level, as mankind had been forced to once more become part of the eco system. Mankind was not so fearsome without the aid of the technology that had helped them to develop such a stranglehold on all the resources of Earth for so long.

The President sat in the Oval Office and stared out the window at the devastation that had ensued following his decision to destroy the Worlds Fair. He could see the planes falling from the sky and sat in tears as the advisers ran around him in total confusion. They had been so quick to push the destruct button on the dream but what they hadn't realised was they had started with their hatred was the final countdown to the complete loss of life as we know it.

A few years later far across the galaxy Marshall was sat in his new laboratory. He had quickly settled into his new life and had developed parts of his brain of which mankind never even knew existed. He had rapidly discovered that there was no need for computers as the brain could calculate much quicker than any processor and it could also run background programs to solve problems whilst you got on with other things. The most important development for Marshall was the ability to speak to anyone via the mind. He could tune into anyone on the planet and have a discussion with him or her. He could also use spare brainpower on the planet as people slept. It had turned out that the dream process was merely a screen saver, which covered the fact that the brain was waiting for instructions. Once people were asleep Marshall could use this immense computing power to solve problems, expand ideas or invent things. Occasionally an idea would come out of someone dreams and it could be developed to its potential. Marshall often thought how mankind had missed out on this and felt sorry for the ones he had left behind for he knew that some would have grabbed this with both hands, the Professor would have been right at the front of this queue trying out this incredible development not of technology but of the brain.

Often he would talk to Frank about Earth and try and distinguish what was mans own work from the alien technology. It was during these conversations that Marshall found out that the history of earth was not as it would seem. Frank told him of all the various links over the years and how they had helped mankind to develop.

"You see Marshall", said Frank on one late night chat, "You were nothing more than hairless apes before we spoke to you. Yes, you showed potential but it would have taken many millions of years to develop that far. Probably longer than Earth had the ability to sustain life" chortled Frank.

"The Earth only has about four million years in which to sustain life and the rate of development of a new species is painfully slow, we helped to push you along and better yourselves before the time ran out. That is why we were desperately trying to form a link between the planets so that in the future no race on Earth may ever die out again due to planet failure."

Marshall would sometimes laugh at Frank's use of language, it was sometimes like talking to a computer as the facts were presented bluntly and without emotion.

"What do you mean again?" asked a startled Marshall on that early Martian night.

"Well, Marshall, you see the Earth has been inhabited before, on several occasions in fact, and each time they have died out due to the natural progression of the Universe. Your people discovered many clues over the years and each time gave them your own unique history. Unfortunately most of the time you were miles out!" laughed Frank.

"Well give me an example!" requested a now confused Marshall.

"The pyramids were a landing port for a civilisation which died out about one million years before yours was even evolving, the people of Ankor Wat were a fascinating culture which grew up out of the jungles and presented us with the first intelligent life on your planet. Long before any of these the Ark people built Stonehenge which was an incredibly precise transmitter which enabled them to have basic communication with the peoples of the moon."

"Peoples of the moon!" exclaimed Marshall "surely that is a joke!"

"Not at all" replied Frank adding, "They were a race which could happily live in the vacuum of space and survive the solar flares that strike the unprotected moons surface. However they were low in population and no matter what they tried their numbers dwindled to zero, and before they could develop fully they were gone. Your very own moon missions saw the buildings they left behind but your leaders had no idea what they were looking at. If they had actually read the transcripts that had been left behind then the history of Earth would have much clearer for all of you. At the very least you would have known how to switch on Stonehenge and not just look at it like it was a load of old rocks!" Frank made himself laugh with the last line of his incredible statement.

Marshall couldn't take too much of this information and would often break the conversation off before he became confused and sometimes a little angry at mans ignorance of Earths real history. Frank would always finish the conversations with the same statement:

 "What we didn't realise was how bloodthirsty your race was! In a way I am glad you didn't link properly otherwise we would probably have a war on our hands!"

Marshall would always sadly have to agree with this as he remembered the President sending two planes to destroy him as he sat in the Skyride high above his home soil.

From time to time Marshall would look down on Earth and wonder what could have been. Mankind, as he had found out, had always had the potential to be something marvellous. It could have been a shining beacon in a dark corner of the universe, but always showed a great desire to destroy. The people of earth had always been incredible but they just didn't know it. Often as he looked he would see them struggling to survive off the land without the technology that had been taken for granted all their lives he would think that they had the one thing that had always been there and was more powerful than any computer. It was sat in everyone's head and the population of Earth had only ever used about five per cent of its power. The brain as it turned out was the only thing that was ever needed and if utilised properly, as Marshall now was doing, was more efficient than all the processors that had ever been made.

Within two hundred years mankind had reinvented the wheel and discovered how to make fire. They had formed societies amongst the rubble that used to be bustling cities and the population of the planet had reduced down to below one million. The total reliance on technology was such that when it was removed most of the population of earth simply couldn't cope. Once the pre-packed food had run dry off the shelves and people had to fend for themselves it was a very rapid decline into chaos and disorder. For a few years man did his usual routine of fighting and forming gangs and when this didn't work many more just gave up. In those first few decades the population was decimated by infighting and starvation as society crumbled. The survivors slowly began to learn how to open their minds to the world and live off its resources. The natural balance of man and nature slowly harmonised and people learnt to live off the land and not destroy the environment and more importantly each other. Slowly the people of Earth began redeveloping as a race of people who used force as a very last resort and learnt to live in harmony with each other. These new people slowly restored a faith in mankind by the others.

One late night Marshall was enjoying a delicious meal with Frank. They were celebrating the fact that Marshall had been installed as the new manager of The Department of Interplanetary contact. The thinking behind this appointment was that Marshall was an alien life form and would be better able to contact other fabulous new worlds that were being discovered everyday. The technology that linked Earth to them was now a network of transport, which had not only linked planets but also galaxies. Marshall looked to Frank and felt the need to ask some searching questions, as was normally the case when he relaxed a little.

"Was it worth all the effort over the years with mankind?"

"Yes and No!" replied Frank, before adding "We learnt an awful lot off your better men, especially the likes of your Professor and the prodigy that was Tesla. They were incredible, insightful people and taught us as much as we taught you. They drove us on to keep trying to link up. But when I think of the weapons and destruction man caused I think it was not worth it…". Frank tailed off the conversation, as it was obvious the sadness of the many innocent people who died at the hands of his misused, innocent inventions played hard on his conscience.

Marshall inquisitively turned to his mentor Frank and asked:

"Do you think we will make contact with them again?"

Frank paused for a moment before replying

"One day they will be ready Marshall, then we will reveal ourselves from behind the fence"

Epilogue

Ten Thousand Years in the making

Winston lived in a small settlement just off the coast. He would spend his days helping around the village and trying unsuccessfully to be a great hunter and provider like his father. Winston often played on the fields near his settlement. He was allowed to play now but would often be told by his father that one day he would have to join the hunt to help out with the feeding of the residents of the ever-growing village.

On many evenings, when he was sat near the fire, his father would tell him great stories about the village and how it stood on an ancient site where many people had once lived. He would tell stories of horseless carriages moving by magic and strange men in flying machines who would swoop like birds over the oceans to far away islands. Winston would sit and listen to these fanciful stories and as he got older would look on as his father told the same great fireside stories for the other children in the village. Winston's' mother would often come out from their hut and tell his father to stop filling the children's heads full of his fanciful stories. Winston loved the stories and would often dream of flying like the men in the stories that his father had told him about.

When Winston was not helping his Father his play would take him over the fields towards the sea where his favourite place was a beautiful meadow lined with trees and leading all the way to the sandy beached seafront. The area always seemed so peaceful and Winston would go there to escape his ever-busier duties in the village.

Just beyond the trees there was a large grassy area in which no one ever played. Winston would often ask his father what was in this area and he always told him to stay away because it was dangerous and strange things had happened there. Being of the age where adventure is the only thing that drove him, Winston would often go right to the edge of the trees and look through at the area beyond. The view from the tree line looked onto a silver fence which wrapped around from the coast and over onto the coast the other side. This fence was as frightening as it was mysterious to Winston and over the months that followed he slowly built up the courage to go nearer. Winston asked his father about the fence and he was informed that it was a village that had 'gone wrong' and had caused the seas wrath that would be unleashed on any unsuspecting person who dared to go beyond its borders.

One hot summers day Winston's inquisitive mind got the better of him and he slowly approached the fence and placed both his hands upon it. The silver metal felt cold and hard against the hot sunny day. The fence was much taller than it looked from the trees and towered above him as the silver wall gave way to the blue sky high above him. After that first time, and no longer frightened, Winston would often play near the fence and would enjoy the peace as other children looked on from the trees in total bewilderment after repeatedly telling him to move away from the fence because they had been told, by their parents, that it was dangerous.

One late summer day Winston was playing near the fence at his usual game of trying to fly like the butterflies and birds by taking off from the grass near the base of the fence. His game would involve him running along the bank near the fence and launching himself into the air whilst furiously flapping his arms, he would fall through the air and land in the long grass that would cushion his fall. He had often convinced himself that he was getting better at flying and this explained his determination in this seemingly endless, and sometimes painful, task. It was after one of these failed flights that when he landed in the grass his feet didn't make the usual thud but a metallic clang. Winston got up and furiously brushed himself down whilst cursing and rubbing his now throbbing ankle. He finally looked to the ground in an attempt to try and discover what he had landed on. He eagerly looked through the long grass and after a little searching he could see the remains of a metal sign. He worked the metal sign free from the soil and after brushing the dirt from its surface he could quite clearly make out some strange markings on it. He had seen the symbols before in the few ancient documents that were held by the elders of the village but he, along with these elders, could only guess at there meanings.

Before returning to the village he carried his sign to his favourite spot, under the shadow of a large tree, and began to copy the strange symbols into the damp soil with the tip of his trusty walking stick:

"Welcome to Chicago 2020" he slowly wrote in the soil.

Printed in Great Britain
by Amazon.co.uk, Ltd.,
Marston Gate.